About the Book

It all started with a sexy selfie.

Texted to the wrong number.

Oops.

Not my finest moment—but I have nothing to be ashamed of.

She thought I was no better, and I quote, *than the knuckle-dragging douche-bags she was never dating again.*

It was a stupid dare from a girl I'd met online, but since she'd given me a fake number, I didn't feel bad that my interests were suddenly focused elsewhere—on the fiery and sharp-tongued, Peyton that I found myself sparring with over text for the rest of the evening.

The following day, my case of mistaken identity came back to bite me in the banana.

When I strolled into the office, I was introduced to Peyton as the new client I needed to win over. The Peyton, in case you're not tracking.

And let's just say she had my *full* attention.

Brains? *Check.*

Beauty? *Oh yeah.*

And the best part? She hated me on sight.

Dear God, do I love a challenge.

Let the games begin.

CHAPTER ONE

Josh

I smile down at my phone at the message Butter-flyGirl6 has just sent me. We've been talking in that *getting to know you to see if we're compatible* lingo for the past three nights, and tonight looks like we'll graduate to dirty talk. *Perfect.*

Her profile says she's looking for Mr. Right, and I honestly wouldn't mind playing that part for the right woman. But so far tonight, her flirty tone suggests she's looking for Mr. Right Now. *And I'm completely down with that scenario too.*

She's asked me what I'm wearing.

She wants to know my favorite positions.

She's curious if I can go all night long.

We moved on pretty quickly from the hobbies-and-interests portion of the chat, but hey, I'm not going to complain.

The last message she sent is her cell phone number, along with a note saying *Let's take this to text, if you know what I mean.*

Oh yes I do, you sexy little butterfly. I know exactly what you mean.

After working my ass off to continue building my company for the past year, I'm a man on the edge. I have my limits, and the desire to pillage and plunder my way through the New York City singles scene is a sharp throb of need that can't be contained any longer.

With one of the biggest opportunities of my life coming up, you might think I should focus on buckling down and stop chasing that wonderful warm spot between a woman's thighs. And the thing is, you'd be right.

It's just . . .

This dry spell can't go on, and that's why I'm scrolling through that dating app—you know the one. It's not even really for dating. It's for hookups.

And while that's not usually my style, Exhibit A is the monster in my pants demanding to be fed, so I'm willing to make some adjustments, both literally and figuratively.

But, hey, I'm also a big believer in giving a woman what she wants. And this woman, this sexy, flirty, naughty ButterflyGirl6—who I've been chatting with for the last three nights via a dating app— has asked for a dick pic.

Look, I'm going to be blunt here. I've never taken a dick pic before. It's not that my second-favorite organ isn't photo worthy. It absolutely is. It's a goddamned work of art, if I do say so myself.

But I still haven't captured its glory on candid camera.

It's just that, well, dick pics are a little uncool. Right? Generally, I pride myself on being a gentleman when interacting with women. And maybe I'm a little old-fashioned.

Sure, I get that sexts and dirty pictures are part of the dating scene these days, but I've found that there are few true surprises left anymore, and undressing a woman you've never seen naked before and exploring every inch of her body is one of them. I'd presume the same applies to a lady. So,

I do enjoy leaving that aspect of dating until, you know, the actual date.

From my spot on the leather couch in my spacious living room, I slide down my boxer briefs, my cock already conveniently in a semi state. And let me tell you, I look pretty damn good already.

Here we go. Time to lose my dick-pic virginity.

I hold the phone a foot or so above the goods and snap a couple of shots, hoping they do the trick. I suppose I could have googled *how to take a dick pic*, but then I'd have to turn in my man card. Some tasks you just need to dive right into and figure out as you go. Besides, how hard can it be—pun intended—to capture a great shot of a great cock?

But when I scroll through the camera roll, I cringe.

Getting the right angle, lighting, and vantage point to show off my favorite appendage is harder than it seems. Again, pun intended.

I delete the first few trial shots. And by delete, I mean I send them straight to the trash can on the phone, and make sure they are deleted for-fucking-ever.

I realize what my first few attempts were lacking.

I need to be fully hard.

Yup. That's the trick.

I head to my bedroom and flick on the light to reveal a neatly made bed, dresser, and a pile of folded clothes still in the laundry basket beside my closet door.

Settling myself on the bed against the head-board, I smile. My white duvet will make the perfect backdrop for the photo. There's nothing to compete for attention with my junk. Impressive as it is, I don't need anything distracting from the mood I'm trying to set for ButterflyGirl6. And that mood is—*at your service, come and ride me all night long.*

Chuckling to myself, I shove off my boxer briefs and stare down at the prize.

I would have assumed I'd need a few stiff tugs to prep the package, but yet here is my dick, ready to impress our new lady friend.

Note to self—never go four months again without some action. It turns you into a horny teenage boy. Forget the fact I'm a grown-ass man at thirty-four. I have needs. And what I need in this moment? To impress the lovely ButterflyGirl6 so she says yes to my request for a date.

Do I find it a little strange that this woman wants to see my goods before taking a look at my face? Sure I do. But whatever, I'm flexible.

A quick glance in the mirror above my dresser reveals tanned skin, a five o'clock shadow, and a mess of dark hair that I keep a little longer than I should.

Making sure the angle is perfect, I snap a shot. When I check out my camera roll, I have to say I'm pretty impressed with my work.

I hit **SEND** and toss my phone on my night-stand. I can't wait for her reply. I'm sure it'll come any minute.

Any minute now.

Maybe just one more minute.

I check my phone once more. Sadly, it's still silent.

I set it down and head for the shower. When I wander out a few minutes later, toweling off my hair, my phone is buzzing with a reply.

I may or may not have run over to the phone to

see what she had to say about the goods.

When I slide open the message, though, her response isn't what I expected at all.

CHAPTER TWO

Peyton

One by one, all my friends are tying the knot.

No, not right this second, not literally. At the moment, I'm sitting at my kitchen table, waiting for a mug of soup to reheat in the microwave. But it still feels that way because over the last eighteen months, one by one, all my friends have either gotten engaged or married. I have four bridesmaid dresses hanging in my closet, and another two on order for this season's weddings.

Meanwhile, I live with my grandmother, or rather she lives with me, but I'm as single as a serial killer on death row. Actually, that may not be entirely true. Serial killers probably get more action than I do.

It doesn't matter. I'm pursuing my dreams, building an enviable career and nursing my entrepreneurial spirit one sale at a time. But all of that is about to change because tomorrow morning is my big chance. A meeting that can lead to my amazing subscription boxes being taken to the big leagues.

"Soup again?" Gram asks.

Gram is not only my roommate, she's also my best friend and my maternal grandmother. Despite being eighty-two, in a lot of ways she's hipper than I am. She wears those printed leggings that people fight over online and covet—today's selection are a monkey-and-banana print. She gets her nails painted once a week at the salon down the street, and she knows the lyrics to all the songs on the radio. Gram is pretty much a silver-haired badass.

"Leftover split pea," I say.

"One of us needs to learn to cook," Gram mutters under her breath.

And by *one of us*, she means *me*. I've heard her say more than once to herself that you can't teach an old dog new tricks. I also know Gram knows how to cook; she just chooses not to. Not that I can blame her. She raised four kids, was married and widowed twice, and was the epitome of a 1950s housewife. I think it's cute that she's having a late-stage feminist streak. So, soup it is. Or takeout. Building my business, I certainly don't have the time or inclination to slave over a hot stove.

I grab my mug of soup from the microwave and set Gram's inside, punching the buttons for two minutes.

"Thanks, sugar," Gram says, picking up her latest knitting project from the counter.

Thankful to be done with work for the evening, I grab a spoon and set myself a spot at the table. While Gram fills me in on the latest gossip at the senior center, I get to work on my soup. Apparently, judging by the gossip that Gram is dishing out, even the elderly are getting more action than me.

"And when Duncan mixes his penis pills with heart pills—look out." Gram chuckles to herself like this is the most amusing and endearing quality a man can have. And at her age, maybe it is.

And there we have it, folks. My life is officially boring.

As I rinse my mug at the sink and place it inside the dishwasher, my phone chimes from the dining table.

Gram steps outside to check the mail while her soup cools, and I grab my phone to check it. There's a text.

Unknown User: Hey.

Peyton: Um, can I help you?

A few seconds later, a photo appears on my screen.

It takes a moment for my mind to comprehend what I'm seeing. But the realization of what I'm actually seeing, and the number of days since I've seen this particular piece of anatomy, has me slow on the uptake.

So many words flash through my brain at once.

Flesh.

Male.

Rigid.

Engorged.

Large.

I squeeze my eyes closed and take a deep breath. What in the world? Who in their right mind sends a dick pic to a complete stranger? And why did this very well-endowed stranger pick my number out of all the possible numeric combinations that exist?

Swallowing a sudden lump in my throat, I peek open one eye. Its size is . . . enviable. There's no denying that. A freaking baseball bat would have Freudian-level jealousy issues.

Unknown User: That what you wanted, baby?

Peyton: And goodbyeeee.

What kind of freak is this guy? That's just creepy. *Ew.* No matter how attractive said penis actually is, and mind you, as penises go, his is actually a handsome one, that's beside the point. Unwarranted photos of this nature are exactly why I don't date. Men are just gross.

Unknown User: What? Seriously? It's not that bad.

Something inside me seethes. The unwanted-peen-shot-sending population of men need to be put in their place.

Peyton: No, it's not bad at all. But what the hell? Why would you send ANYONE this shot unsolicited?

Unknown User: You asked me to send it!

Peyton: Ha. Try again, buddy. I definitely did not in any way, shape, or form ask for this pic.

Unknown User: Wait. Fuck. You're not ButterflyGirl6, are you?

Peyton: Who? No. I'm definitely not.

He doesn't reply right away, and a dry chuckle escapes my lips. Serves him right that someone gave him the wrong number.

But she's kind of missing out on quite a nice schlong, to be honest.

I should be offended. Unsolicited dick pics are aggressive, inappropriate, and downright rude. But strangely enough, I'm not offended. I'm kind of . .

. intrigued.

My interest gets the better of me and I dare another glance at the offending member. My cheeks redden in a way that has nothing to do with the warm soup in my belly and everything to do with my lack of a sex life.

Confronted by that . . . *thing* staring back at me, I have so many questions.

Namely, how does he haul it around all day? Isn't it uncomfortable? Loads of other inappropriate questions like *Do you only date sword-swallowers?* flit through my brain. But I refrain from actually typing them out in a text to Mr. Dick Pic.

Thank God.

My kitchen table is hardly the place to be musing over such things. I move to get up, but before I can, Gram enters the kitchen and glances over my shoulder.

"What's that, a ham hock?" she asks.

I slam the phone screen-down on the table. "What? No."

I shake my head firmly, hoping to end this conversation before it starts. But given that I'm the only thing of importance in Gram's life, she's bound to be on this like a dog with a bone.

"Leg of lamb?" She gives me a curious look as she heads to the counter to make herself a cup of tea.

"No, Gram. Don't worry about it."

She shrugs, setting a teacup into a matching saucer. "Whatever it was, it looked delicious. So juicy and tender, I bet it melts in your mouth. I thought you were looking up recipes to cook for me."

Letting out a groan, I shove the phone inside my pocket and rise to my feet.

Gram eyes me curiously. "You're flushed, dear. Are you feeling well?"

Nodding, I feel my phone vibrate in my pocket and place my hand protectively over it, eager to get out of the kitchen. "I'm fine. It's sort of warm in here, is all. I think I'm just a little anxious about tomorrow."

Tomorrow. The biggest day of my life, and here I am sexting with some stranger.

"Get some rest. Maybe a nice warm bath. I'll bring you some tea once you're settled," she says, her blue eyes crinkling at the corners. "While you're in the tub, you should really look up some more *meat* recipes like what was in that picture. I think I'm going to dream about that side of beef, or whatever it was, instead of that vegetarian stuff you keep feeding me."

I squeak out a nonsensical reply and scurry toward the stairs, taking them two at a time because I seriously need to get out of this room. And according to my own grandmother, I seriously need to get laid.

Safely inside my bedroom, I shut the door behind me and tug my phone from my jeans pocket. Sinking onto the edge of my mattress, I read the new message.

Unknown User: Shit, I'm so sorry. Despite the aforementioned erection, I promise I'm harmless. Please accept this photo of me from the third grade as proof. My apologies.

Staring down at the most adorable photo of an awkward eight-year-old with gapped teeth and a bowtie, I let out a snort laugh. Who the hell is this guy? Someone extremely bad at flirting, that's who. Some poor girl clearly gave him a fake number, wanting him to fuck off, and now I'm the object of his attention. Lucky me.

Peyton: OMG. That just made this entire exchange ten times more awkward.

Unknown User: Yeah, I guess it did. Shit. Clearly, I'm not very good at this whole thing.

Peyton: What? Being human?

Unknown User: The name's Josh. Seriously, I'm really sorry.

Peyton: My name's Peyton. Apology accepted—as long as you don't whip out that flesh wagon again and assault me with it.

Unknown User: Only if you ask nicely.

I laugh. How sad that this is the most flirting I've done in over a year.

Peyton: Well, good night then, Josh.

Unknown User: Good night, Peyton.

I decide against asking him how exactly he plans to sleep while World War III rages between his legs—because, holy hell, that erection looked painfully swollen, but I do no such thing.

Instead, I busy myself with having a mug of sleepy tea with Gram, brush my teeth, and then review my notes for tomorrow's presentation before I climb into bed and dream of being devoured by a giant one-eyed python.

CHAPTER THREE

Josh

I walk down Madison Avenue toward my company's office fifteen blocks away. After living in Manhattan for nearly a decade, I still love it just as much, if not more, every day. This city energizes me, and so do the people. Today, the walk offers the added bonus of time to shake off the memory of my royal fuckup last night.

In the light of day, I have to physically try not to cringe at the memory of the exchange. What else *can* I do? Though I do wonder who Peyton is.

As I pass a coffee shop, waving to the barista who makes a kickass espresso, I wonder if Peyton is an artsy gal, serving up lattes to customers and putting a smile on their faces. On the next block, as I nod a hello to the curly-haired lady with three teenagers who runs the organic cleaners where all my suits are pressed, I wonder if Peyton might be a married mom of three. *Oops*.

But the other thing I'm damn curious about is this—did she secretly enjoy not only the pic, but our exchange? Hell, that picture was a fine shot. I still have no idea why ButterflyGirl6 gave me a fake number. I'll bet the number belongs to a friend of hers, and she wanted to see if I'd actually do it, and maybe now ButterflyGirl6 is cursing herself for missing out on the ride of her life.

I won't hear from her again, though. Last night after the major screwup, I returned to my dating app, deleted my profile, and erased all photographic evidence of my member from my phone. Some close calls you don't need to experience twice, and I definitely don't want to tempt fate. One wrong sender receiving an up-close-and-personal view of my private parts is more than enough, thank you very much.

By the time I reach my office, the walk through the harried Manhattan crowds has reset my mood. I stuff my earbuds into my pocket, run a hand down my tie, and stride into the building, ready to tackle the day and forget all about last night's little error.

Big error.

I mean, it is big, if I do say so myself.

It's time to focus on business, and honestly, my job is one of my favorite things.

Inside the office, I say hello to Irene, our receptionist. "How are things with your son? Did his Little League team win the championship?"

She smiles and adjusts her red glasses. "They did. We went out to celebrate at Famous Ray's."

"Every celebration should include pizza. It's a law, you know."

"It's one I follow judiciously," she says with a wide grin.

When I reach my office, my assistant, Toby, runs in, frazzled and breathing hard. "Josh!" Everything he says is in exclamation points; even breathing for him is exciting.

"What can I do for you, Toby?"

Panting, he drags a hand through his wiry hair. "Brody called me! He tried to call you!"

I frown, then snap my fingers. "I was listening

to a podcast. I might have hit DO NOT DISTURB by mistake."

Toby grabs his stomach. "Brody ate wheat last night! By mistake!"

I cringe. Brody can't go near the stuff on account of the world's worst allergy. "That sucks."

"And he wanted you to take his morning meeting with Wish Upon a Gift."

A new boutique is slated to open a few blocks from our flagship store on the Upper East Side, and that's why Brody has been hunting for new partnerships to give us an edge.

I nod and flip open my laptop. "Right. Sure. He sent me the file the other night, and I glanced through it."

Toby points wildly. "She's in the conference room right now. He said it's vital that you fill in for him!"

I push my hands down so he knows to cool his jets. I've handled plenty of meetings before. This one isn't going to be an issue. I stand, clap Toby on the back, and tell him I'll be there in five minutes.

Toby darts out the door, his feet clopping down the hall.

I review the file quickly, refreshing my memory of what I already scanned the other night. Then I slide open my phone and find about 547 texts from Brody.

They include phrases like *too dizzy to live, I'm only ever eating fruit, wait—is there some new wheat-based fruit that's secretly trying to kill me, my life is the worst.*

And then there are the more business-like ones . . . *new client with a subscription box that's all the rage, seal this deal like the deal-sealing mofo that you are, this company is the toast of the town—but not wheat toast, we want to partner with them like a magnet wants all the metal in the world, like my dick wants all the ladies in the world.*

Yeah, he's a bit all over the place.

I text him back.

```
Josh: It's under control. Sorry
to hear that some wheat kicked
your ass . . . again.


Brody: *middle finger emoji*


Brody: Also, thanks, man.
```

I head to the conference room, cringing when I overhear Toby telling the prospective partner how he had to help his roommate give her long-haired tabby a pill last night.

"I had to wrap him in a towel like a burrito," he says.

The woman laughs. "That's why I like dogs. "You can just trick them with a little bit of peanut butter."

Her voice is pretty, sweet and melodic, and I wonder if the face matches.

I step into the conference room and . . . *holy matching face of an angel*. The Wish Upon a Gift woman is hotter than sin.

The brunette perched in a conference chair is smiling at my assistant, showing off the prettiest lips I've ever seen. She wears a black-and-white dress and looks like a cookie I want to bite. Which is a thoroughly inappropriate reaction.

I remind myself to expunge inappropriate thoughts from my mind. My dick got me in trouble last night. No way is that sneaky bastard getting me in trouble now. But, fuck me, I seriously need some action.

She and Toby turn to me.

"This is Josh Hanson! He's my boss! And he's also a rock star in one-on-one basketball. He kills me every time we play!"

Um, we played once. But Toby's right. I did destroy him.

I give him a self-deprecating grin. "You played valiantly. It was an even matchup."

The woman stands, revealing long, toned legs that I do my best not to stare at because I'm not an asshole who objectifies women—especially not women I want to do business with. But right now, I'm waging an internal battle between my dick and my brain. And the longer I stare at her, the closer my dick is edging to victory.

Not cool, man. Not cool.

I focus on her eyes and that's a whole new challenge, because they're sky blue, a gorgeous contrast to her lush dark hair. She stares at me a little longer than I'd expect, like she's studying my face.

I extend a hand, and after hesitating for a second, she takes it.

"Nice to meet you, Josh." She swallows a little hard on my name, like it surprises her or is hard to pronounce. "I'm Peyton."

I blink. What the actual fuck? What are the chances she's the same Peyton?

Slim to nil, right?

Has to be.

Because there's no fucking way she can be the same Peyton. Her name isn't a common one, but this has to be a weird coincidence.

As we shake hands, her gaze drops to my hands and she stares for an awkward beat or two. Like she's cataloguing them now too. Like she's doing the math—big hands, big feet, big . . . all over.

When she looks up and meets my gaze, the chance of her being Peyton just surpassed one hundred percent. Red splashes across her cheeks. Her eyes are huge and wild. Her face is the picture of embarrassment.

I cringe, and Peyton coughs. She recognized me from my childhood photo . . . not the dick one, obviously.

"Nice to meet you," she says, as if she's straightening out her words and trying to speak for the first time in ages.

"Good to meet you too, Peyton." Trying to keep my tone as even as I can, I turn to Toby. "And thanks again. Especially for the cat tales."

He laughs as he leaves, and when Peyton and I take our seats, there's a tiny smile on her face too.

"Cat tales," she murmurs with a little laugh.

"I personally prefer taking my pills with peanut butter," I say, hoping to use humor to defuse the situation. We both know what she has seen, and it's hella awkward.

This situation is all kinds of fucked up, and I need to unfuck it. Stat.

She stares at me, her nose crinkling. "So, last night . . ." She shakes her head, frustration etched on her face.

Which means it's time for me to launch into a full-court apology. After all, we can't risk losing her business to someone else.

"Look, Peyton. I'm sorry. I had no idea who you were. Your number must have been on my phone because of the file Brody sent me. I did not in any way, shape, or form intend to send you that picture. I'm so sorry."

It's the only explanation. I mean, how else

could I have mistaken her number for Butterfly-Girl6's?

Peyton lets out a heavy sigh and presses her hand to her face as if checking to see if the temperature is still high. "I seriously can't believe you sent it to me."

I sigh as well. "I can't believe I did either."

"And I can't believe you sent me your elementary school photo too."

Yeah, that was weird. I see that now.

I frown, scrambling to fix the problem. "In my defense, I was trying not to seem like an asshole who sends unsolicited dick pics."

She holds up a hand to stop me. "Can we just not talk about that picture?"

"The kid pic or the junk shot?"

She raises her gaze to mine. "Both. Can we have a whatever you call it in basketball? A mulligan?"

I chuckle. "That's a golf term. But we can just call it a do-over."

"Yes, we need a do-over," she says with an earnest nod. "We need to pretend it never happened

and go about this meeting like we've never met before today."

Yeah, good fucking luck with that.

CHAPTER FOUR

Peyton

"I can do that," Josh says with a confidence I don't share. He grabs a sheet of blank paper from the conference table, crumples it up, and tosses it over his shoulder. "There. Done. Out of sight. Out of mind."

I give him a shaky smile.

If only it were that easy.

Over the last eighteen months of growing my business, I've done a hundred things that I never thought I could do.

Quit my job to pursue my dream? *Did it.*

Build my own website from scratch? *Done.*

Interview with a popular blog for a piece high-lighting my accomplishments? *The post was published last Wednesday.*

But hold eye contact with this perfect ten of a male specimen without letting my gaze venture down to sneak a peek at that bulge? Is *this* really going to be my breaking point?

"Brody and I were really excited to meet you. Thanks again for coming in. Can I tell you a little bit about Wine O'Cock—I mean, Clock?"

I make a small noise of agreement, hoping that he thinks I didn't catch his rather *large* faux pas. "Please."

What is this life and why am I living it?!

"We've been looking forward to meeting you. Let me tell you a little bit about where we're heading these days . . ." As Josh shares details on his company's direction, I'm amazed he can segue so seamlessly, bridging the gap from the ridiculously awkward to cool-as-a-cucumber CEO.

His confidence is a little surprising, to say the least. You'd think accidentally exposing yourself to a potential business partner would knock a guy down a few pegs. If anything, he should be blushing and I should be the one smirking, not the other way around. But I guess if you know you've got a work of art between your legs, it's hard to be humble. Now that I think about it, "humble" might not even be in Josh's vocabulary.

"Tell me what you think about all that," he says, waiting for me to share my own thoughts.

What I think is that it's time to save this deal. And that's what I intend to do.

"I love all those partnership possibilities," I say, then tell him the story of my company.

I launched my subscription box service on a hope and a prayer, and now all the hard work, the late nights replying to manufacturer emails, and negotiating costs and securing clients, is finally paying off. My little boxes could be on retail shelves all over the city and the East Coast, all the places where Wine O'Clock has been expanding.

This deal could mean so much for both Gram and me. A nicer apartment, money for proper health insurance, savings for my retirement. Maybe even a little fun. I hardly remember what that word is anymore.

But now this?

No. No. *No.* That's not what today is supposed

to be about.

Today is about my business, about his luxurious boutique wine shops possibly carrying the product I've created. My gift box subscriptions have been bringing in a solid stream of revenue, but a deal with this company would take my business to a whole new level. This could be my key to success . . . I just wish the person holding that key wasn't *ham-hock-cock Josh*. Gram is going to die when she hears about this.

If only I could delete that picture from my memory the same way I should have deleted it from my phone, but a girl can't just forget her first dick pic, especially one as museum worthy as that. With its wide tip and veiny shaft . . .

No. Bad Peyton. Focus.

The effort it's taking me to think about anything other than that beautiful gift between his legs should count as cardio. My heart rate is up, that's for sure. I take a deep breath and straighten my shoulders.

"It's a tiny speed bump," he says, smiling at me again. "We can move past it, right?"

"I would hardly call that tiny."

I realize the error in my words immediately. My throat goes dry, threatening to close up completely. I make a strangled noise, and Josh's smile fades.

"Can I get you water? Did anyone offer you something? Let me grab you a water."

He's already risen to his feet and is halfway to the door before I'm able to respond.

"Sure, um. A water would be . . ."

He steps outside the conference room and is already calling to Toby for two *aguas, por favor*. No one in the office appears to be Spanish, so I have no idea why the sudden shift. Unless he's completely forgotten where he is. This isn't tenth-grade Spanish class, that's for sure.

But when Toby responds with some Spanish phrase of his own and a good-natured laugh, and I realize it was Josh's attempt at humor. Lightening the mood.

Part of me wonders if I should use this distraction to slip out the door right now. Forget the whole thing and move on with my life. Maybe this isn't my big break. Maybe this is a detour, or a giant flashing neon sign from the universe.

But how is that fair? I've worked so hard to get

to this moment, I can't let a little thing—okay, a rather *big* thing—like this stand in my way.

It's like the universe is laughing at me, telling me not to take myself so seriously. Or maybe that I should have followed Gram's advice to go out and get some action. Because Josh, *fucking hamhock-between-the-legs Josh*, is way too delicious for words.

It certainly doesn't help that his confidence is sexy as all get-out, just like everything else about him. He wears that sharp black suit like he's doing it a favor, and his necktie may as well be the yellow brick road that my eyes are skipping down, making their way to his . . .

Straightening my shoulders, I accept the cool bottle of water Josh offers when he returns. I take a deep drink of it as he slides into the seat across from me again, holding his own bottle.

"I'm sorry you missed meeting Brody. He had an unexpected health thing come up."

"Is he okay?" I ask, recapping the bottle and setting it aside.

Josh mirrors my movements and nods, his expression turning serious. "He'll be all right, as long as he stays away from any more gluten."

A smile spreads over my face of its own accord. "I've heard gluten can be quite terrifying at times."

"You really can't be too careful in those situations."

Yeah, this guy is super confident and, honestly, quite sweet in his attempt to defuse the awkwardness. I've read about the owners of Wine O'Clock online, and they're known not only for building an enviable business in a little over five years' time, but also for an excellent track record with business partners.

I can completely see why. He's so smooth about this whole debacle.

So that means he has smarts, looks, confidence, and humor?

God help me.

Folding his hands on the table in front of him, Josh leans closer. "Peyton, let's get down to the nuts and bolts of this, shall we?"

And my face goes beet red again.

CHAPTER FIVE

Josh

Nuts?

Seriously, Hanson? Of all the words in the English language, you choose nuts?

But hey, on the plus side, she hasn't seen the boys, just their leader.

Even so, I need to keep this meeting above the belt, including my own damn thoughts. I offer Peyton another apologetic smile. Time to get this deal back on track.

"Want to tell me more about your company?"

"I do. I really do. I would love to tell you about Wish Upon a Gift."

Her tone shifts instantly when she mentions her business, making me even more keen to hear her pitch.

I smile. A perfect, professional smile, as I cross my legs and fold my hands in my lap. I'm a motherfucking gentleman, not a junk-shot-sending caveman. "I want to hear all about it, Peyton."

The only way to get past this mixup is to focus on business.

Not on her pretty face.

Not on those gorgeous eyes.

And definitely not on that dark hair I want to wrap around my fist and yank on it hard.

Four fucking months . . . that's what's wrong with my libido. It's not operating in its normal over-drive. No, today, it's at fucking warp speed. This is what happens when your own hand becomes your closest companion.

I conduct a full mental sweep, keying in on the words Peyton is saying.

"I started Wish Upon a Gift when my best friend was pregnant and overwhelmed. I started making little gifts for her to help her in the final weeks, and then once the baby was born too."

My smile widens. "That's very thoughtful."

"Thank you. I've always loved showering friends with gifts, to be honest. It was really fun to do that for her. I heard from other new moms that they also, not surprisingly, felt overwhelmed. And I thought about meal services and food-delivery subscriptions, but I also wanted to do something that wasn't just utilitarian."

I nod, liking her story. "Yup. I'm with you. Utilitarian and practical is good, but little luxuries and treats are too. We love our luxuries in the wine business."

A gleam of excitement lights up her eyes. "Exactly. I wanted to move beyond the practical and curate gift boxes for date nights, or for no occasion at all. Something that can make an ordinary Tuesday special—a box of chocolates, massage oil, maybe a bottle of wine."

"You've done well with it," I say, recalling Brody's notes. "A lot of people these days are wanting to give more authentic gifts. The heyday of the gift card is starting to wane, and consumers are wanting to put more thought into their gifts."

"Exactly! People just default and give each other gift cards, but a lot of people still want to give meaningful gifts to friends and loved ones, and that's where I wanted to take Wish Upon a Gift."

She reaches into a cavernous bag on the floor and takes out a few boxes to show me. Her excitement is infectious. She's passionate and delighted and truly seems to care. More than that, these boxes are fantastic. They look classy, but fun.

We chat more about terms, and options, and how this would pan out. And since Brody made his wishes clear, there's only one thing left for me to say.

"Peyton, we'd love to work with you. And I'm confident we can continue a business relationship, while at the same time putting this awkward situation behind us."

Her blue eyes sparkle. "This is a tremendous opportunity."

I clear my throat. "Fantastic. I'll email you more details on the terms."

But as she stands, her chair rolls a little closer and her knee brushes mine while we rise. I glance down at her legs, then back up.

It was less than a second of innocent contact, but we both seem to fixate on that moment more than we should. When my eyes meet hers again, her breath catches, her cheeks pinken with bright spots of color, and a flush travels up her neck.

I can feel it in the air . . . all the possibilities. Hauling her into my arms and kissing the lipstick off her.

I bet it would be fantastic. Hot and wet and unraveling.

And then I remember that less than twenty-four hours ago, Peyton was the recipient of a candid shot of my goods, and now we're going to be business partners. I'll have that memory in the back of my mind every time I talk to her, and I'm afraid I'm going to sabotage this deal.

Brody will kill me if I fuck this up.

CHAPTER SIX

Peyton

As Josh and I walk together toward the elevators, I want to dance for joy, to squeal and punch the sky. But there will be time for that later. Right now, I need to be professional. Just because I've seen this attractive man's johnson doesn't give me the right to leer at him. So I put on my best game face and pretend that my stomach isn't tied in a gigantic knot.

"I think this will be a great partnership," I manage to say.

"I do too. And I promise to keep it professional." Josh extends his hand to me.

As I stare down at his open palm, my mind immediately wanders to how his long, thick fingers would feel against my skin.

Jeez, am I really so starved for sex that a handshake will make the floodgates open up? Playing it safe, I opt to place a business card into his palm instead.

"Absolutely professional," I say on a trembling exhale, hoping I can actually live up to it.

Josh pockets my business card, his mouth curling into his signature half smile that sends a spark of heat dancing up my spine.

"It'll be fine," he says, pausing just past the reception area. "Even in unusual situations, I try to do my best to close a fantastic deal."

I look down in an effort to conceal the blush I feel spreading across my cheeks.

Closing a deal? Is he suggesting something, or am I reading too much into things? Is this another example of his terrible flirting?

"I'm excited to be in business with you." I'm doing my darnedest to be businesslike, but when I repeat in my head the words I just spoke out loud, they sound strangely flirty too. Was something in the bottled water?

"Business is indeed exciting." There's a hint of something more in his blue eyes, a spark even. "Thank you again for coming in. And feel free to call—or even text—with any questions about all the contract paperwork."

"I'm sure I'll be in touch soon." I give him my best *everything is great and I'm totally not attracted to you at all* smile. "Do you have a business card I could take?"

He produces one from his suit coat pocket and places it in my hand. His fingers graze my skin, leaving a trail of heat in their wake.

"Th-thank you, Josh," I murmur.

Clutching the card in one hand, I give the team behind him one last wave before I breeze past him and head straight toward the elevator bay. Part of me is worried that my speedy exit will come off as rude, but the rest of me knows the longer I stay in this office, the higher my chances are of making a fool of myself.

As the elevator doors close, I allow myself one final peek. Sure enough, there's Josh, loosening his tie and shooting me that devilish smirk.

Bastard! It's not fair that he accidentally flashed me his privates, yet I'm the one who's frazzled.

Once the elevator starts moving, I finally release all that composure I've been faking and take the first deep breath I've managed all morning. I thought the last eighteen months of building this business were difficult, but I have a feeling that things are about to get a whole lot harder. No pun intended.

I want my business to succeed, and that means I have to keep my eyes on the prize and *off* Josh's bulge. If he says he can keep it professional, then I can do the same. And I know when I get my first big paycheck from this company, the restraint will all be worth it. I have to do what I have to do, and unfortunately, what I have to do isn't Josh, as much as every part of me would really like it to be.

A notification pings my phone. Happy hour with Sabrina and Libby at five.

Thank God. I sure could use something strong to curb these nerves and help me forget about Josh and all of his gorgeous parts.

At a few minutes to five, I walk over to our favorite bar, Speakeasy. Once inside, I glance at our favorite corner table by the window.

Sure enough, Sabrina and Libby are already there, laughing, each of them well into their first martini of the night. No doubt they're chatting about details for their weddings this summer.

It's weird to be the only one out of the three who isn't engaged. Don't get me wrong, I'm beyond happy for both of them. I just wish I at least had someone to bring as my plus-one.

As I approach the table, I spot a grapefruit martini already waiting for me, and I grin. These girls just know me.

"Look what corporate America dragged in!" Libby teases as I snag the seat across from my redheaded friend. "Did they keep you late offering you millions and millions of dollars?"

I roll my eyes. "Not even close. But things did go pretty well, for the most part."

"Of course they did." Sabrina grins, somehow managing to look younger than her thirty-one years. Someday, I swear I'm going to get her to give up all her skin-care secrets. "Because you're a rock star."

She holds up her martini, and Libby and I follow suit, clinking our glasses together.

"To Peyton livin' her dream," Libby says before taking a nice long sip of her martini. "So, tell us everything. Do you think the deal is going to work out?"

"I still have a lot of paperwork to review," I say, tapping my bag full of the legal documents I'll be spending the next week poring over. "But things are looking pretty good. They seem very excited about the boxes, but I don't think it's going to be particularly easy working with Josh. He's one of the owners."

"Why? What's up with him?" Libby asks. She's an account manager at an ad agency, so I knew she'd be quick to make sure I was being treated fairly as a client.

I take a sip of my tart beverage and release a slow exhale. "What's up with him is that he's beyond gorgeous, and he totally knows it. And he knows that *I* know it. Rock meet *very* hard place."

"Oh no, being offered a deal with a major corporation *and* having to stare at some sexy man candy all the while knowing you're getting paid for this torture. Sounds *horrible*," Sabrina teases, pulling out her phone and punching in the company website. "What's his name?" She's already scrolling through the management team's head shots and bios.

"Josh Hanson."

Libby leans over Sabrina's shoulder as she scrolls, then stops on Josh's head shot. Their eyes widen, and for a second, I'm worried I'll have to pick Libby's jaw up off the floor.

"Holy shit," Sabrina whispers, zooming in on Josh's angular jawline. "Are you sure this is the co-owner and not some model they hired to try to win you over as a client?" She turns her phone to face me, as if to get confirmation that this is, in fact, the guy.

The picture hardly does him justice, but I'd recognize that cocky smile from a mile away. If only they knew I could one-up this image with the "self-portrait" of Josh I have on my phone.

"That's him."

"I presume this means that after the deal is closed . . . well, that you're going to go after that, right?" Libby props her elbows on the table and leans in toward me. She's the more sexually adventurous of my friends.

Normally, I adore that about her, but right now? I need her to stop talking. ASAP.

"Yeah, right. That would be super inappropriate."

Libby makes a face like she just sucked on a lemon. "What's inappropriate is how long it's been since you've gotten laid," she blurts out a little louder than I'd like.

Sabrina raises her glass and drinks in agreement. "Cheers to that. Please tell me there's been somebody, anybody, since that pencil-dick ex of yours."

Sheesh, first Gram, now Sabrina and Libby. My total lack of a sex life may as well be front-page news at this point.

It's my own fault—working nonstop, thinking I can exist entirely on work, takeout dinners, and my favorite dirty Tumblr page at night when sleep won't come. It's been a gross mistake on my part to remain in a self-imposed state of celibacy for the better part of two years.

The worst part about it all is that they're totally right. I need a man. A red-blooded male with a functioning cock. And stat.

Josh's cock looked pretty damn functioning.

Shit. I'm woman enough to admit that it won't

be Josh's cock in my future. That much is certain. It can't be, no matter how much I want it to be. If I have to choose between success and my sex drive, Tumblr will always be there for me with no strings or awkward meetings attached.

But opportunities like this might not be.

CHAPTER SEVEN

Josh

I'm eight blocks into my walk home from work when my phone buzzes with the message I've been waiting for all afternoon.

Brody: How'd the meeting go?

I knew this text was coming, but that doesn't mean I have a good answer to it. I pause, stepping out of the flow of foot traffic to stare at the text for a second before I respond.

Josh: Funny story . . . *eggplant emoji*

As quickly as I've typed the text, I delete it.

I can't let Brody know about my screwup. But I can't ignore him either, so I go for a vaguer approach.

```
Josh: Went great. Work on get-
ting the gluten out of your sys-
tem. Talk more tomorrow.
```

When he responds with a thumbs-up emoji, my whole body relaxes. Thank God, I've got more time to figure out my strategy in dealing with Peyton and our business plans.

Having my business partner double as my best friend has never been a problem before, but then again, I've never been one to mix work and sex. I'm a professional, after all, not some horny intern who doesn't know the rules of the workplace. I've been deliberate about keeping my hookups far, far away from my work life. Because they're just that—hookups. A way to blow off steam here and there.

If this were a normal dating-app match gone wrong for me, Brody would be laughing his ass off with me over drinks—of course, beer for me and tequila for Brody's gluten-intolerant ass. But this situation is about as normal as a three-headed pit bull, and as dangerous too. Brody spent weeks hunting down the right business to collaborate with before he landed on Peyton's genius little company. He'd have every right to kick me in the nuts if he knew I nearly fucked up his deal by sliding dick-first into Peyton's DMs.

When I'm back in the apartment, I grab a beer from the fridge and open my calendar app to check my availability this week. Amidst all the weirdness, I didn't accomplish half the shit Brody had wanted me to get done with Peyton at this meeting. Which means I'm going to have to set up another meeting soon.

My dick perks up at the thought, but I will it to stand down. This isn't the time for my dick to start acting up, and it's certainly not the girl, no matter how goddamned sexy she looked during our meeting today. What I'd give to have those pretty, pouty lips open up for me. She's already seen what I'm packing. I could have asked her if she wanted a taste.

Nope, nope, nope. Get it out of your system now, dude, because this won't fly.

This potential partnership could be next level for our company, so the only thing that's allowed to be hard around here is the work I'm putting in. Nothing else is an option.

With work on my mind, I settle in on the couch with my beer and tap open my email. Maybe logging a few more hours will serve as a cold shower for my wandering, dirty mind.

First on the to-do list: arranging another meeting with Peyton.

I open a new email and start carefully crafting my message. *No slipping up and accidentally saying* nuts *again, Hanson.* Time to pull out all the stops on all the least sexy corporate terminology I learned in business school. For good measure, I work in the word *synergy* so she knows I'm not messing around.

The email ends with the suggestion of a lunch meeting tomorrow. I give her the link to the site for the restaurant in our office lobby. It's not exactly Michelin-star-worthy food, but it's upscale, and it beats being stuck in that conference room with her again. After what I've put her through, the least I can do is expense a panini for her.

Hardly a minute passes between pressing SEND and the ping of a response. Her reply is short and sweet.

From: Peyton@WishUponAGift.com

Confirming for noon tomorrow. Looking forward to it.

—Peyton Richards

I stare at her email signature, finally putting a last name to her first. Peyton Richards. PR. Like public relations. Like in nightmare. As in the kind of scandal we could have on our hands if word of my first-impression picture ever got out.

If Peyton was looking like a ten yesterday, today she's looking like infinity.

No, seriously. With the way that little black dress hugs her body, she's looking as curvy as an infinity sign.

I got to the restaurant a little early to be sure we snagged a table before the lunch rush hit. It was a good move based on how packed the place is, but a bad move based on how late Peyton is running. Normally, I'm a stickler about being on time, but one look at her sculpted legs revealed by that dress and all sins of her tardiness are forgiven.

Her dark hair is pulled back at the nape of her neck, and as she scans the restaurant for me, I can't help but linger over the delicate column of her neck. It's impossible not to imagine myself nipping at it as my hands grip her plush ass. And it's hard not to wonder about all the other soft places she might let me bite.

Fuck me. I have to stop this now.

"Josh." She brightens and waves to me when she spots me across the crowded restaurant.

I give her a nod of acknowledgment to beckon her over to the table. Not gonna risk standing up and showing off a clothed and napkin-covered version of the picture she has of me.

"Sorry I'm a little late." She checks the time on her phone and her eyes bug out. "Wow, okay, a lot late. I had to drop Gram off at the senior center."

Once she's settled in her seat, I pass her a menu, letting my gaze settle on the pretty pink flush the fall air has left on her cheeks.

"Nice of you to drive her. Do you spend a lot of time with your grandmother?"

The pink in her cheeks deepens two shades. "Um, actually, I live with her," she says meekly, peering at me over her menu. "She's in good health, but she shouldn't be living on her own. And we're actually kind of best friends. I know, it's sort of weird."

I sip at my lemon water without so much as raising a brow. "I don't think it's weird at all. Nothing is more important than family."

Her embarrassment morphs into pleasant surprise. "I agree completely. Do you see much of your family?"

I give her my typical spiel about being the only Hanson left in Manhattan, how my family is mostly upstate and all that, but I'm interrupted when the waitress comes by to take our orders. Turns out, I was right yesterday when I guessed she would be a panini type of gal. I go with my usual salad with a filet of salmon on top, batting away my concerns about having fish breath. Hopefully it will reinforce the fact that I'm not planning on swapping spit with anyone today. Problem solved.

"I knew it." Peyton folds her arms over her chest, a satisfied grin twitching on her lips. "I knew I had you pegged as the health-nut type."

I smirk. I should have known she'd already be passing judgment on me—and she also said *nut* today and I don't think she even realized it.

"Nah, you should see how much ice cream I go through. If I had a roommate, they'd think I was going through a breakup every weekend with the number of pints of fudge brownie I polish off by myself."

Peyton's brows furrow into a tight little *V*. "Is that why you were on that dating app? Looking for a rebound after a breakup?"

All right, Richards. I wasn't gonna go there, but since you took it there first . . .

"No breakups in a few years. I've been single a long time," I say, leaning back in my seat. "I'm on that dating app because I like talking to attractive women."

"Like ButterflyGirl6?" she teases.

"Like you."

The words come out of my mouth before I think it through, and I immediately regret letting them slip. *Shit.* I barely covered my ass during yesterday's meeting. Haven't I done enough damage already without using pickup lines on this girl?

Before I get a chance to pull my head out of my ass, the waitress comes by and sets our food in front of us. Peyton stares down at her panini, avoiding eye contact with me.

Shit. I blew it. How in the hell am I supposed to explain this to Brody? I start racking my brain for other small businesses I know in the area, anyone I could turn to who could potentially be a backup when this deal inevitably falls through.

Once the waitress is out of earshot, Peyton mutters something under her breath as she fiddles with the toothpick in her sandwich.

"Pardon me?" I ask, bracing myself for whatever horrible name she's about to call me.

"I said you're not so bad on the eyes yourself." She finally looks up at me, batting those baby blues in my direction as her mouth widens into a wicked smile.

Heaven fucking help me. I'm starting to think I might not be strong enough to not constantly think of Peyton in every inappropriate way I can if she keeps saying things like that.

"Um, so did you get a chance to look at any of that paperwork?" I blurt out, making no effort to smooth over the abrupt subject change. "I'm happy to answer any questions you may have."

Thank the Lord she doesn't call me on my bullshit. Instead, she transitions seamlessly from flirty Peyton to business Peyton, which, frankly, is equally as sexy. But at least now the fuck-me eyes are gone, and the beast behind my zipper can calm down for half a second.

The rest of our lunch is business as planned. I discuss our projections to expand across the state in the next few years, and how her product offerings would play into that plan. She nods along, taking small, polite bites of her sandwich and challenging me to keep my eyes off her mouth.

When the bill comes, I slap down my company credit card, a visual reminder for both of us that this was a lunch meeting, nothing more.

"You hardly touched your salad," Peyton says as I pull a twenty from my wallet to leave as a tip.

She's right. I took two bites of salmon, three tops.

"I wasn't really hungry." I shrug, hoping she can't tell I'm totally lying.

Truth is, I'm starving. But what's the point in choking down a salad? I know what I really want, what I've really developed a taste for. And she's sitting right across the table from me.

CHAPTER EIGHT

Peyton

"**S**o, they're just starting to pass out the bingo cards, and I swear, Duncan is already grabbing my thigh under the table!"

There's embarrassment, and then there's being trapped in a pedicure chair while your grandma loudly describes a sexual encounter with her senior-discount-eligible boo-thang. Never a dull moment with Gram.

"So Duncan says to me, 'Listen, Marge, do any of those bingo prizes really look better than heading back to my room?' Right in front of everybody at our table! I could hardly believe it!"

Our nail ladies are chatting in a language I don't

understand, no doubt complaining about having to listen to this senior-center romance that Gram has been weaving for the last ten minutes.

I can't say that I blame them. Being ultra-close with your grandmother seems endearing until you have to hear the kind of details no granddaughter should be subject to. And this is far from the first time. I think Gram hopes that if she keeps sharing her geriatric romantic trysts with me, I'll eventually have some hot gossip of my own to spill on my love life.

Despite her efforts, I've had nothing to share. For the last year and a half, the only men in my life have been the ones placing orders for subscription boxes as gifts for their wives and girlfriends. When I started this business, I didn't think about the fact that it pretty much limits me to exclusively dealing with men in committed relationships. Well, them and gorgeous account managers, apparently. And if Josh is in the habit of sending nude selfies to ladies in chat rooms, I think it's safe to say he's on the market.

"What about you? Any exciting news in your life, sweetie?"

I don't have anything that can match the level of steaminess of that bingo story, but I'll try my luck at filling Gram in on my business updates. "Well, I had my first one-on-one meeting with my account manager yesterday."

Gram wrinkles her nose in distaste as her pedicurist scrubs at her bunions. "Not that kind of news. Fun news. News about sex, my dear." That last part was said with a little more gusto than I'd prefer.

The pedicurists immediately start talking faster after Gram's outburst, and I die a little more inside.

If only she knew that Josh *is* my fun news, and my sex news, if I'm being honest. But if I admit to Gram that I have a major lady boner for my account manager, she'll never drop the subject, and having her constantly nagging me about him isn't going to help this whole *keeping it professional* thing. There has to be some other "fun" news in my life I can spill to throw her a bone.

"Oh! Sabrina and Libby took me out to happy hour the other night. We haven't racked up that kind of bill on martinis in months."

Gram perks up in her seat. "See, that's fun! Any special occasion, or just a fun girls' night out?"

"We were celebrating my big meeting," I admit.

And I've lost her. She throws her head back into the headrest of her cushy pedicure chair, either in frustration or just to get comfortable, I'm not sure.

"Meeting this, account manager that. It's hard to live vicariously through my granddaughter if all you do is work."

"I'm not working right now, am I?" I wiggle my toes, splashing a little bubbling water out of the pedicure basin. My nail lady gives me a stern look.

"Only because I dragged you out here to do something nice for yourself for once. If it weren't for me, you'd never stop checking your darn email."

With a steady hand and perfect precision, my nail lady begins to apply perfect, thin coats of the deep red polish I picked. When was the last time I had a pedicure? Probably not since the last time Gram booked us both appointments and forced me to go.

Okay, maybe always putting my rest-and-re-laxation boxes before myself has meant slacking on some of my *own* R&R, but it's also brought me a lot of opportunities. If I hadn't worked so hard, I never would have gotten this offer that could end up completely changing my life. And if I hadn't gotten this offer, I may never have met Josh face-to-face, although I'm still not sure if that's a good thing or not. According to my friends, it's a great thing and I should nail him as soon as the deal's set, but they don't always have the best advice. I'm still not over that time that Libby told me blue lipstick was in style.

For my business, it's definitely a good thing. Josh knows what he's doing and how to help me build my brand. Still, my nerves were totally out of control going into my meeting with him yesterday—a professional meeting in a café—yet it felt too much like a date for me to keep calm.

Plus, with how cocksure he came off the first time we met at the office, I expected to be dealing with a bullheaded negotiator, but that was hardly the case. He made everything seem so easy, steering the conversation like the perfect dance partner. He led us smoothly but firmly through the agenda while offering plenty of room to accommodate my questions and suggestions, even throwing in a joke here and there. He's easy to talk to, smart . . . and don't even get me started on how attractive I find him.

"So this big fancy business deal. Do you think it's going to work out?"

Gram's voice is kind of flat, but I appreciate her trying to show some interest. It's not that she's not proud of me and all the work I've put in, it's just that it's all she's heard me talk about for the last year and a half.

"I really think it might," I say, then mentally add *if I can just ignore how completely hot Josh is*, a task that seems more and more impossible by the minute.

If dating your coworker is a big no-no, making a move on the man in charge of the business deal that could make or break my company is completely out of the question. But how do I just totally write off the chemistry between the two of us? I stare down at my bright red toes as if they will somehow reveal the answer to me.

Can't I just have my own ham hock and eat it too? Adulting is so hard sometimes.

CHAPTER NINE

Josh

Friday is chest-and-triceps day, my personal favorite muscle group to hit. I save the best workout for the end of the week to add a little icing onto the cake that is the two days of freedom ahead of me. I could be biting into that cake by now too, if it weren't for my slow-ass lifting partner.

From my vantage point as Brody's spotter, I have the pleasure of watching every bead of sweat form on his forehead as he pounds out reps on the bench, huffing and puffing the whole time. Dude's been out of the gym for a few measly days with his little gluten incident, and suddenly he's acting like he's never picked up a barbell in his life.

"Come on, slacker. Pick up the pace," I tease.

Don't get me wrong, I'm happy my best friend is no longer on the brink of death by bread, but I was sort of looking forward to a solo weight-lifting session after work. The plan was to pop in my earbuds and get in some quality detox time.

As if the misdirected dick pic wasn't enough of a weight on my shoulders this week, we've got our biggest corporate event of the year tomorrow night. That's right, instead of plopping my ass on the couch with a beer and a movie on my Saturday night, I'll be wining and dining the company's corporate partners. So a little time to myself to decompress was in tall order.

No such luck. Instead, I've spent the better part of an hour spotting Brody and evading his questions about yesterday's lunch meeting. And as hard as it is dodging his nosiness, it still doesn't count as a workout.

Brody lets out an enormous grunt as he finishes off the last rep of the set. "Shit, dude," he says between pants. "I've gotta be done now, right?"

"You wish. You've got one more set left."

Brody's groan of displeasure is so loud that several of the girls in the yoga class across the gym turn their heads in our direction. Probably to make sure that sound didn't come out of some dying animal. Nope, just Brody.

I nudge his shoulder with my knee. "Your girlfriends are staring, dude."

While Brody doesn't love chest-and-triceps day, he is the number-one fan of the all-female yoga class that's held here on Fridays. I don't exactly mind the view myself, to be honest. I'm not some pig who's trying to pick up girls while they're getting in a workout. But if they're going into downward dog right in front of me, a guy's not exactly gonna cover his eyes.

But today, for what has to be the first time in history, I've got no interest in the legging-clad asses on display across the gym. There's a different ass on my mind lately. An ass that, unfortunately, I'm supposed to be *keeping it professional* with. Not that my dick seems to be getting that message. And with the way Peyton looked at lunch yesterday, I wouldn't be surprised to find out that she and my dick are teaming up against me.

But it's not just my junk that's Team Peyton either. I have to keep my brain on the world's shortest leash to make sure my thoughts don't go wandering back to her.

I'm not sure what it is, but there's something about the two of us that just clicks. Not once during our lunch together did I have to scrounge up some small talk or feign interest in something she was saying. Talking to her felt like second nature. I can't say that about anyone I've chatted up on a dating app.

I intended it to be a business lunch, so I have no idea why it felt like a date. The best kind of first date too, the kind you only see in the movies, where there are no awkward pauses or drawn-out silences. The kind where the couple is laughing and smiling and teasing each other like they've been doing it for years. That was Peyton and me.

I'm centered again by the clang of the barbell hitting the rack.

Shit, I zoned out and haven't been spotting Brody. Lucky for both of us, he didn't need any help—and he didn't die. He finished the set, no problem. Well, maybe a little bit of a problem. His face is red as fuck.

"Jesus, shit. *Now* I'm done?" It's less of a question and more of a plea.

I nod, putting the poor sucker out of his misery. "Yeah, you're done. Go towel off before you flood the place. I've got one set left."

Brody peels himself off the bench, leaving a shimmering, sweaty outline behind. "I'm never skipping the gym again," he grumbles under his breath as he heads for the towels.

While I load the forty-five-pound plates onto the bar, I find myself wondering if Peyton is into muscles. More specifically, I wonder if she's into *my* muscles. What did she say about me at lunch yesterday? *You're not so bad on the eyes yourself.* Paired with those bright blue eyes she locked on mine? Have fucking mercy.

Conjuring up the image of her in that little black dress sends a jolt of interest to my crotch. *Shit.* I fucking knew I shouldn't have worn gray joggers.

It takes a solid minute of visualizing Brody's sweaty forehead until my dick relaxes back into place. Just in time for Brody to get back too. I let him wipe his disgusting sweat angel off the bench before I slide under the bar and pound out my last set of the day, throwing in a few extra reps for good measure.

"Shit, man. Do you always lift that heavy?"

I mutter something about adrenaline and focus

on re-racking the weights. Brody doesn't need to know what, or who, has my blood pumping a little extra lately.

Once the weights are back in place, Brody tilts his head in question toward the basketball court, but I shake my head. We'd originally planned on shooting hoops after our workout, but Brody's snail pace put an end to that idea.

It's been a long day, and I'm eager to get home. I've got errands to run before our event tomorrow, and still have a tux to pick up. It will definitely be a full evening of schmoozing wine-drunk business partners. God, I hate working the big events. That's the sort of stuff that Brody is better at. Me? I prefer working with people one-on-one.

And just like that, an idea pops into my head. An idea I like a hell of a lot. I decide to run it by Brody.

"Should we invite Peyton to the event tomorrow night?" I ask as we head for the locker room. "I know it's technically for existing partners only, but I think it'd be a good chance to show her how we run things. You know, impress her with the full swanky treatment. Let her see what she could be getting herself into."

Brody mulls it over for a second, then shrugs. "Not a bad idea. I say we go ahead with it. You're her point of contact. You should be the one to extend the invite. Although, who knows if she's even free. It's pretty last minute."

"True," I say. But it's still worth a shot.

The first thing I grab once I open my locker is my phone, and I quickly compose a text to Peyton asking if she's available tomorrow night. She responds instantly that her calendar is completely empty.

Perfect. I forward her our digital invite, but this time, she doesn't respond so quickly. I send her another text, letting her know it's cool if she wants to bring a plus-one with her. If she has a plus-one, I guess it's better that I find out now before I get too carried away with my low-key obsession with her.

A watched phone never rings, or something like that, so I grab my body wash and hit the shower. When I come back, no messages. Also, no Brody. He must have bounced, clearly not as interested as I am in whether we'll have an extra guest joining us for the event. Makes sense. At an event where we'll be entertaining over a hundred guests, what difference does one extra person make?

The bigger question is, why the hell does it make such a big difference to me?

Just a week ago, I was prowling the digital dating scene, searching for a girl of the ButterflyGirl6 variety. I needed someone to help me blow off the year's worth of steam that had built up from being all work and no play. One night of fun, that's all I was looking for. One and done and back to my regularly scheduled program, dividing my time between the office, the gym, and the occasional night alone with my right hand. I had things all figured out.

Until Peyton.

And now here I am a few days later, checking and rechecking my phone to see if I've got half a chance of seeing this girl tomorrow night. A girl who, a few short days ago, I never could have seen coming. A girl who showed up in my life, and suddenly my dating apps are completely forgotten, practically developing cobwebs from lack of use.

As I'm toweling off, my phone buzzes in my gym bag. I can't snatch it up fast enough.

```
Peyton: See you tomorrow. *smi-
ley-face emoji*
```

There's no one in the locker room to see the enormous smile spread across my face. She's said nothing about a plus-one, so I have to hope that means she's coming alone.

Let the seduction game commence.

CHAPTER TEN

Peyton

"**C**ome on, Gram! Our ride is here!"

I put on my favorite gold chandelier earrings and checked my makeup one last time in the foyer's full-length mirror. Josh's last-minute invite to a formal corporate event might have thrown me if not for my stockpile of bridesmaid dresses. Luckily, this emerald-green dress from a wedding last winter still fits like a glove. It's modest, to the knee, and has cap sleeves. It looks particularly good paired with my game face. I'm ready to network like a boss. Because, well, I am a boss.

"Don't get your panties in a bunch!" Gram squawks. "I'm comin'!"

I peer out the window to make sure the sleek

black town car in our driveway hasn't left without us. I was perfectly satisfied with driving ourselves or taking public transit to the event, but Josh insisted on sending a company car to drive us there. I was tempted to ask if he sends town cars to the homes of all their prospective business partners, but it seemed safer to just assume this is standard practice.

Moments later, Gram descends the stairs rocking a bright-red ankle-length dress speckled with gold sequins. Where the hell she got it, I haven't a clue. I'm just glad she agreed to be my plus-one.

When Josh mentioned the invitation was for me and a guest, I entertained the idea of bringing either Sabrina or Libby, but I wasn't entirely certain I could trust either of them to play it cool with what they know about Josh. One poorly timed joke about a certain account manager's impressive third leg, and I might as well start writing a eulogy for my deal with his and Brody's company. *Dearly beloved, we are gathered here today to mourn the loss of a potential business deal, ruined by an inappropriate dick joke.*

With Gram in tow, I head down the driveway and slide into the back of the town car. I may not know much about cars, but I know this one is leagues above anything I've ridden in before. Heated seats in the back? Does the Queen of England normally ride in this thing?

"Well, isn't this swanky?" Gram clucks her tongue, running one age-spotted finger along the leather seats as we pull out of the drive. I guess the driver already knows the address of our destination. "You owe that Josh fellow a huge thank-you."

I force a smile, trying not to react to Gram using *Josh* and *huge* in the same sentence.

"Yes . . . it was, um, very thoughtful of him," I manage to say.

Luckily, she doesn't bring him up again, too dazzled by the view of Central Park at night to make much conversation. Traffic is actually cooperating for once. How very unlike Manhattan. It's like all the stars have aligned to make this a special night for Gram and me. We make impressive time on the drive to the hotel, and after a quick thank-you to our driver, we twirl through the revolving doors and into a whole different universe.

Holy bougie. Is this what it's like to make it in corporate America? *Deep breaths, Pey.*

"What a place," Gram says in an astonished voice.

I can't help but agree, numbly nodding my head as I look around.

The lobby looks fit for a king—from the sleek, sparkly tile to the modern chandeliers, everything is gold. Even the bright red Wine O'Clock banner hanging over the hors d'oeuvres table boasts flashy gold lettering. A dance floor is set up with a handful of couples stepping along to a band playing a familiar jazz tune. Everyone else is flitting about the room like a bunch of windup dolls in suits and ball gowns, sipping from wineglasses with the company logo frosted on the side.

I scan the room for a familiar face, with a particular eye out for Josh, admittedly, but can't seem to find anyone I know. My game face is slipping away, and the butterflies inside my belly are trying to make an escape.

I feel more than a little out of my league with so many business professionals all gathered in one place. Apparently, working from home for the past two years in my pajamas has taken its toll on my social skills. Maybe I should just tell Gram that I'm not feeling well and head out. Josh would understand, I'm sure . . .

"Free wine? Count me in!" Gram says, giving the air a fist pump. Then she takes off power walking toward the open bar, leaving me alone at the entrance to the ballroom.

I should have known I'd lose her to the social scene. She's outgoing and personable when she's at the senior center, but at this event, it's like Gram's at a frat party. I'm sure she'll have made a few new friends before the night is through.

I weave through the crowd, following in her path until I find her, elbows propped up on the bar and chatting it up with a cute twenty-something bartender. He's grinning at her as she fills him in on my big deal.

I give him an awkward wave. "Hi."

Gram places one arm around my shoulder and pats it encouragingly. "This is her, my hotshot granddaughter. And she's single." She winks at the bartender, who is obviously a little horrified.

Welcome to the club, dude.

He's close to ten years younger than me, and I'm operating under the assumption that he's gay, unless my radar for that kind of thing is off, but this doesn't stop Gram. She gives me a little shove in his direction.

"I'll have a glass of cabernet," I say, hoping to

end this little matchup attempt ASAP.

"Green dress and red wine, huh?"

I turn, glass in hand, to greet the low voice behind me.

"Those are complementary colors, you know."

It's Josh. He's dressed in a black tuxedo that's tailored so perfectly to his broad body, it's almost sinful. His hair is styled without a strand out of place, and he smells freaking divine. He obviously has to dress well for work, of course, but tonight he looks like someone plucked him straight from the red carpet. I don't think he's ever looked better.

Well, except maybe in the picture saved on my phone.

"Red and green. Christmas colors," I say, taking a sip of wine. It's warm and velvety, just like Josh's voice.

"Well, I wouldn't mind seeing you wearing a big red bow under my tree."

My mouth falls open, and Josh's lips hint at a smile. There are dozens of company partners within earshot. Is he seriously flirting with me right now? My cheeks burn, probably turning the same color as my wine.

"This must be the famous Gram I've heard so much about." Josh gestures toward my grandmother, who turns around in mid-swig of wine upon hearing her name.

One look at Josh, and her eyes widen to the size of golf balls. I'm pretty sure the bartender has been immediately forgotten.

"Sure am." She laughs, extending the hand that isn't gripping her wineglass. "And you are?"

"Josh Hanson. I'm in charge of the collaboration between Wine O'Clock and Wish Upon a Gift. It's a pleasure to meet you . . ."

I clear my throat as Gram hangs on to the handshake for a moment too long. *Great.* Even my grandmother is smitten.

"Gram is fine," she says.

When she finally releases his hand, I try not to feel a little jealous that my grandmother has touched Josh more than I have. Then I silently correct myself. *He's not mine to touch—he's just a guy I'm working with. That's it. Keep your damn panties on, Peyton.*

Gram narrows her eyes at Josh. "How old are you?"

He smiles wryly, clearly amused by her. "I'm thirty-four."

"And you're single?" she fires out next.

Holy hell, what is with this interrogation?

"Very," he says as he briefly meets my eyes, and the tingles in my belly spread south.

Gram's lips press into a line as she considers this information. "Thirty-four, huh. You're no spring chicken. Why don't you have a wife? Are you batting for the other team or something?"

My eyes widen in horror but Josh only laughs, the rich, deep sound throbbing through me and leaving something warm in its wake.

"That's a very good question. I guess the reason I'm single is because I prioritized building my company over pursuing a relationship, but I hope to rectify that in the future. And to answer your last question, I most assuredly love the company of a beautiful woman." He shoots a quick glance my way, and I inhale sharply.

Gram nods once, seemingly pleased by his answer. "Good. So you're not one of those hit-it-and-quit-it player types, are you? You're looking for something real?"

Josh nods. "I'm not a player. And absolutely, someday I would love to settle down."

As my stomach twists itself into a gigantic knot, I feel Josh's gaze rake over me. *Please don't hold my crazy grandma against me*, I think, fake-smiling at him through my horror. I had no idea she was going to unleash the Spanish Inquisition on him.

As I search for conversation topics that don't start with *Gram, this is the proud owner of the ham hock you caught a glimpse of*, the band transitions into their next song. Gram wiggles in delight. Clearly, she knows this one.

"It's lovely to meet you, Josh, but I just can't miss this song. You'll have to excuse me."

I take a deep breath and watch her sashay toward the parquet dance floor at the center of the ballroom. I'm not sure if Gram dancing will embarrass me more or less than the game of twenty questions we just played, but something tells me I'm about to find out.

Pausing in her mission only long enough to grab some random older gentleman in a navy suit to dance with her, Gram shimmies off toward the dance floor, disappearing out of sight into the crowd. I hope to someday have half the confidence with men that my grandmother has.

"Your grandma is wild. That's the CEO of one of our biggest whiskey distributors." Josh laughs, shaking his head in disbelief.

That laugh. Low and deep . . . it does something to me. Clearly, I'm a little overdue for some male interaction if a *laugh* is what's lighting my fire.

"Never a dull moment with her," I say, distracting my lips with my wineglass so I don't do anything stupid, like try to take a nibble from his Adam's apple that's peeking out above his knotted black tie. "I'm really sorry about her asking you all of those personal questions. I'm not sure what got into her. Actually, scratch that, I know exactly what's gotten into her. She has this idea that I need to be set up and find a good man. Before you arrived, she was trying to make a love connection between me and the bartender."

Josh's eyes settle on my mouth for just a moment, before they lift to mine once again. "I highly doubt you have any trouble finding a male companion, Peyton."

Then his gaze cuts over to the bartender, and he smiles. "But I don't think the bartender is quite your type—or that you're his."

I grin and take another sip of my wine, enjoying the pleasant warmth as it settles in my stomach.

We're quiet for a moment as we sip our drinks, our focus straying toward the dance floor. Gram is clearly having an amazing time with the man in the navy suit. He actually knows how to dance, and they're making it look fun.

"She's one of the most incredible women I've ever met," I say, watching her in awe.

Josh takes a step toward me, close enough that the toes of our shoes almost touch. "You must take after her, then."

I open my mouth, looking for a quick or witty response, but I'm at a loss for words. He's not making this *keeping it professional* thing easy. I manage to squeak out a "thank you" as my gaze shifts to my feet. Our feet. The toes of our shoes look like they're kissing, and I'm not-so-secretly jealous of them.

"Excuse me."

An unfamiliar voice brings my focus back up. A tall, broad-shouldered man with well-combed blond hair is holding out a hand to me.

"Would you like to dance, miss?"

Unsure of the protocol here, I glance from Josh to this blond stranger, then back to Josh. His jaw is clenched, his chest slightly puffed. Is he . . . threatened by this guy?

"She's with me," Josh finally says, grabbing my hand and lacing my fingers with his. My palm nestles into his, a perfect fit.

"My apologies, I beg your pardon." The blond stranger gives us an apologetic nod and, with no further questions, turns to offer his hand to another potential dance partner.

"I'm with you, huh?" I smile up at Josh, squeezing his hand ever so slightly, just enough to remind him he's still holding on to mine. And to my surprise, he doesn't let go.

"Sorry, that came out wrong. I just meant work wise, we're here to pound it out, right?"

I chuckle at his failed attempt at a joke while Josh shakes his head.

"Why is it that so much of the business jargon that's used in offices and networking events around the country sounds so perverted?"

I raise one brow at him. "Maybe because it is?"

"Burning the midnight oil." He winks.

"Doing the grunt work," I say, my tone airy and flirtatious, and he chuckles.

"Sliding into your in-box."

"I'm ready to go balls to the wall if you are."

He smirks. "As long as I don't get the shaft."

My smile turns into laughter, and Josh puts on a mock serious face.

"In all seriousness, I think we can get some great penetration for your product, Peyton."

It's all so easy with him. The joking, the small talk, the laughing. It feels like the most natural thing in the world. And something about that scares me a little. Why does the biggest professional thing I've ever had happen and the best-looking guy I've ever met have to intersect? I just hope I play this the right way and don't screw up either opportunity—or worse, both of them.

"That's why we're here, right?" I say after a moment.

He blinks down at me, his smile slowly fading. "You're right. That's exactly why we're here."

I finish off my glass of cab just as the song

crescendos to a big finish. The band announces that they'll be taking a fifteen-minute break, and a smattering of contained applause emerges from the crowd as people wander off the dance floor to get a refill on their beverage.

"We should get out of the way," Josh says. "Everyone's about to flood this bar behind us. Come on, I'll show you the rest of the hotel."

With my stomach still tight with nerves, Josh takes my hand again, leading me through the crowd and down a quieter corridor. As we get farther and farther from the noise, he points out the different amenities we pass like he's a real estate agent trying to sell me the place. He could be reading me the phone book for all I care. Just watching his lips move is all the entertainment I need.

"You know I'm not staying here tonight, right?" I ask as we turn down another hallway. "I don't exactly need to know where the pool and workout facilities are."

"I know." Josh glances my way. "But I needed you to myself for a moment. I'm greedy like that."

My tongue touches my bottom lip, and when I meet his eyes, the heat reflected back at me is hot enough to melt the panties off of a nun.

"You look beautiful tonight."

"Thank you." My voice is little more than a whisper, but, jeez, I'm way out of practice at this flirting thing.

"I don't know what this is between us, Peyton, this chemistry . . ."

I give him a curious look. I didn't expect this tonight, assuming his invite was purely for business purposes. Josh is probably just flirty with everyone. I figured it was his personality, he's so playful and easygoing.

But then his face falls. He thinks I'm rejecting him.

"I'll escort you back to the ballroom, and we can continue working together like none of this ever happened," he says, his tone several degrees cooler than before.

Placing one hand on the lapel of his jacket, right over his firm chest muscles, I hold him in place as I murmur, "I feel it too."

His gaze darkens on mine, and then Josh spins me around until I'm pressed against him, my left hand still pressed against his chest while my right steadies my balance on his shoulder. Slowly, he leans down, bringing his mouth to mine. He pauses for a second, maybe to read my reaction, I'm not sure, and then he's kissing me.

Gently at first, then harder, greedier, as his mouth claims mine in the most intense kiss I've ever had. His hands move to cup my jaw, and his tongue slides over mine. This is everything a kiss should be. Hot. Tender. Passionate.

When he pulls back, my lips burn in longing. *Come back. Kiss me again.*

Josh swivels his head to check that we're still alone, then meets my eyes. "Are you okay?" he says, his deep voice little more than a strained whisper.

"Very." I nod, touching my lips with the pads of my fingers. I can't believe he just kissed me. I can't believe he thinks I'm beautiful.

Before I can process anything else, he grabs my hand again, pulling me around yet another turn. "This way." He reaches for the first door handle he sees. Maybe he has a room here tonight.

When the door opens to reveal a coat closet, we both smirk. Not the most romantic setting, but it's private, and right now, we need privacy desperately, because I'm nowhere near done with that kiss. I lead the way in, tugging Josh by his lapel. The door swings closed behind us, and we collide.

His lips on my neck.

His fingers in my hair.

My hands roaming his broad shoulders.

My heart threatening to leap out of my chest.

As his lips find their way back to mine, he palms my breasts through my dress, his thumbs drawing a quick circle around my nipples. They go instantly stiff at his touch, even with a layer of fabric in the way.

It isn't until I pull back slightly to catch my breath that I notice the firmness of his erection pressed against my belly. Clearly, I'm not the only one enjoying myself.

Oh my God . . . holy chemistry, Batman.

"I thought you said you could be professional, that you wanted this to remain professional," I whisper against his neck, nudging his erection with my hip. "*This* doesn't feel very professional to me."

"I said *I* could keep it professional. I didn't say anything about *him*." Josh nods toward his crotch and a giggle escapes me, louder than I intended. He presses a *shh* into my lips, but I can feel his mouth smiling against me as his lips meet mine again.

"Please stop being so good at this," I say in a half whisper, half whine.

"I'll see what I can do," he says, his lips moving to my throat, and I shudder against his hot breath.

He wants me. Plain and simple. The man who was once just a dirty picture on my screen is now here, in the flesh, and has me swallowing my moans in a hotel coat closet.

And I can't block the embarrassing thought that if Gram knew, she would be so proud.

CHAPTER ELEVEN

Josh

I could have sworn my days of making out in coat closets were far, far behind me. But I'm so fucking glad I was wrong.

If it were anyone other than Peyton swirling her tongue around mine and sucking greedily on my bottom lip, this might feel like reverting to teenage behavior. But there's nothing teenage about the body grinding up against mine. Peyton's tits are full and perky and fill up my hands just right as I palm them, feeling every perfect curve and thumbing her nipples through her dress.

God, this woman. She's smart enough to have built a successful business, but she's got more sex appeal than corporate America can handle. I want her. So damn bad. And the way she's grinding her hips against the ridge in my pants seems like a pretty good sign that she wants me too.

I'm so damn wound up—celibacy will do that to you—that I can't think past this moment.

I won't let myself think about any possible repercussions right now, because I'm sure there are many. This moment feels so right, and I'm not about to stop. Not when she's eagerly kissing me back and rocking her hips against my hard dick.

Fuck. She's testing all my limits.

With my mouth still firmly pressed against hers, I let one hand slip from her breasts to the slit of her dress, testing her limits. She doesn't stop my hand. Instead, she throws her head back, her dark waves spilling down her back as my mouth travels down to her neck.

"Is this okay?" I push open the slit of her dress and brush my fingertips against her inner thigh.

She shudders, a needy whimper tumbling from her lips. "Yes. God, yes. Please."

With her permission, I trail my fingers up her thigh and find a damp bit of silky fabric between her legs. A groan of approval escapes me at the realization she's already wet for me. I run my middle finger along the silk, then twist it out of the way. Peyton's punctuated gasps make my already hard cock go completely stiff.

I can't wait any longer. I need to know how she feels.

Wasting no time, I gently press two fingers deep into her wetness, an entrance that is met with a gasp of surprise and plenty of bucking from Peyton.

"Fuck," I mutter when I feel how tight she is.

"S-so good." Her response is breathy as she clutches my shoulders. Her fingers dig into my muscles, getting a good, stable grip on me.

I like that she's counting on me to keep her upright. I could get used to this side of our business arrangement.

Slowly, I ease my fingers out, giving her clit a few gentle strokes with my thumb. She moans in response, and I'm lucky enough to catch her gaze for a second. Even in this dark closet, her blue eyes absolutely sparkle.

When I begin touching her again, she rocks against my hand and those eyes flutter closed. After a few thrusts, she finds my rhythm and starts tilting her hips against my fingers in time with me, letting my fingers hit a deeper, softer spot within her. It's enough to make both of us moan. My thumb finds her clit again, and her whole body tightens around my fingers. She's close, and suddenly, I've given up all hope of keeping things quiet. There's nothing I want more than to hear her moan, to soak in the blissed-out look on her face as she climaxes.

"Go ahead, angel," I whisper, nipping at her ear. "Come for me, Peyton."

My words push her over the edge.

I curl my fingers inside her and her jaw drops open, a breathy moan pouring out of her as she comes undone. She squeezes her eyes tight, trying to hold herself together, but her muscles clench and pulse until she finally lets out a soft sigh.

It's so damn hot.

I'm not even worried about anyone hearing Peyton's moans. Let them hear. I'd wear Peyton's orgasm as a medal of honor, given the chance.

Well, I take that back. Not under these circumstances. But in a less professional setting? Definitely.

Once I've eased my fingers out of her, Peyton's grip on my shoulders loosens and she finds her own balance again. It may be dark, but I can still see the new stain of pink on her cheeks. It pairs well with the *fresh off an orgasm* glow.

"Wow," she whispers as one hand grips the back of her neck, then floats down so her fingers can intertwine with mine. "I, um . . . I think that was the best orgasm of my life."

There's no stopping the proud smile that spreads across my face. It's not the first time I've gotten that compliment, but somehow, it means more coming from her. And it's been so long since I've shared pleasure like this with a woman. It's good to hear that I haven't lost my touch.

In the momentary silence between us, I can just barely hear the band announce that this will be their last song of the evening. *Shit.* We've been gone way longer than I thought.

"We should get back," we both say in almost perfect unison, then laugh. We've known each other less than a week, and apparently, we can already read each other's minds.

After we've smoothed out our clothes and gathered ourselves, Peyton looks over at me, her gaze drifting to the front of my pants that still sport an obvious bulge.

Her lips part. "Are you sure you're going to be okay?"

I pull in a long, slow breath and nod. The concern in her eyes as she takes me in is equal parts adorable and hilarious. She looks genuinely worried.

"I'll be fine." I'll probably have to jerk off twice later just to get to sleep, but I'll live.

After discreetly adjusting myself, I crack open the door. The coast is clear, and moments later, we're walking down the hotel hallway, chatting as though nothing out of the ordinary just happened.

But *ordinary* is the last word I'd use to describe what just went down between the two of us. Not unless you tack an *extra* in front of it. Because, goddamn, Peyton is extraordinary in every possible way.

Back in the hotel lobby, it takes us all of a microsecond to spot Peyton's grandmother. She's one of the only people left on the dance floor. Well, her and the CEO of Byron County Whiskey. I still can't believe she's dancing with him.

When the song ends, the band gestures to Gram, and the few remaining partiers left in the lobby all applaud. I guess her dancing has caught everyone's attention. Even the caterers set down their trays and clap. The applause dies down, and after a polite curtsy, Gram shakes her dance partner's hand before making her way back to us.

"You missed some damn good songs!" Gram exclaims, laying a hand on her heart as she catches her breath. "What were you two up to?"

"Just work stuff," Peyton says quickly before I have a chance to get a word in.

I nod in agreement, trying to suppress the chuckle building in my chest. Work stuff, eh? Is that what that was, because damn, I'll become a workaholic effective immediately.

Gram must know Peyton pretty well, because the mischievous smirk on her face says she can see right through that lie. "Work stuff? At a party like this?" She snickers. "Whatever you say, dearie."

Peyton is blushing again, but Gram doesn't notice. She's already directed her attention toward me.

"So, Mr. Josh." Gram plants her hands firmly on her hips, her voice suddenly stern. "My granddaughter here keeps hitting me with all this business mumbo jumbo. I need your professional opinion. Do you think she works too hard?"

Peyton groans, but I can't help but laugh.

"Well, I haven't known your granddaughter nearly as long as you have, of course. But I can tell you that her hard work has gotten her pretty far. The partnership we're building between our two companies is, for lack of a better phrase, a pretty big deal."

I pause to assess Gram's skeptical reaction. I guess grandmothers aren't easily won over with the corporate stuff. At least, this one isn't.

"How about I make you an even *bigger* deal?" I say, and Gram scrunches her eyebrows, urging me to go on. "If you're willing to listen to the aforementioned business mumbo jumbo, I'm willing to make sure your granddaughter loosens up a little and has some fun while we're working. Sound fair?"

An enormous, toothy smile splits Gram's face. She puts her soft, pale hand in my rough calloused one, and we shake on it. "We have a deal." She laughs, then turns to Peyton and adds, "I knew I liked this one."

We say our good-byes, and Peyton thanks me profusely for the invite and the town car and "everything else."

It doesn't take a genius to decipher what she's referring to. When my phone buzzes with a text from the driver that their town car is ready outside, I walk them out, letting Gram grip my arm for balance as she navigates down the steep hotel steps and into the back seat.

"It's been a pleasure, Mr. Hanson." Peyton squares up her shoulders and extends her hand toward me.

We're back to business mode, which is for the best, with all the people around. Still, every bone in my body wants to pull her against me and kiss her, to tangle my hands in that dark silky hair and taste her for the second time tonight. But that's just my body talking. Right now, I need to listen to the parts of my body above my waistline. Wherever it is in my anatomy that I store my common sense, I know it's not in my dick. So a handshake it is.

"Text me when you make it home so I know you're safe," I call out as she slips into the car, hoping she knows what I really mean. *Text me when you make it home, because you're going to be on my mind all fucking night.*

The town car pulls away, and I head back into the hotel to make sure I've said all my necessary good-byes. I'm expecting a few investors or corporate partners to be lingering, but instead, I find Brody in the middle of the lobby, tipping the band as they load up. Other than a few caterers who are still cleaning up, the place is a ghost town.

"Pretty successful evening, huh?" I call across the lobby, getting my best friend's attention. I'm expecting a *hell yeah* or some similar agreement, but when he turns toward me, Brody has a look of complete surprise on his face.

"Dude, where the hell have you been? I think I saw you for a grand total of ten seconds tonight."

Guilt churns in my stomach. It's not like I didn't chat with plenty of our partners early in the evening, but once Peyton arrived, all my attention was on her. But Brody would have smoke coming out of his ears if he knew that.

"Oh, sorry." I give him a grin. "Did I spend a bit too much time with our investors and not enough time with my best friend that I see every day?"

Brody rolls his eyes and laughs, indicating that I'm off the hook for being MIA.

"Do you know if Peyton from Wish Upon a

Gift ever showed up?" he asks.

It's an innocent question, but that doesn't stop my heart rate from climbing. I scrunch my brow, trying to look like I have to think about whether I saw her or not, then snap my fingers in realization.

"Yeah, I saw her. We chatted for a few minutes. She seemed pretty impressed. Sorry, dude, I should have sent her your way since you two haven't met yet."

"No big deal on the introductions. I'll see her another time. I'm just glad that she enjoyed herself."

My memory flashes back to that look on her face, the way she trembled on my fingers as she rode out the wave of her orgasm. The best orgasm of her life, according to her. If only Brody knew exactly how much our potential business partner enjoyed herself.

But he can't know. Just like he can't know that I was sloughing off my duties as the co-founder of our company tonight.

It's a little chilly out since the sun has set, and my apartment isn't within walking distance from here, unlike the office. Something about wearing a tux on the subway seems wrong, so I call a car to take me home. When I slide into the back seat, I give the driver terse responses to his usual small-talk questions. He catches the hint pretty quickly that I'm in no mood to chat tonight. There's too much on my mind that I need to sort through, and almost all of it has to do with Peyton.

We both said we'd keep things professional, and we both went back on our word. So now what? I'm not about to let my work performance suffer because I can't keep my word.

But I've got another promise to uphold now too. I told Gram that I'd help Peyton loosen up and have a little fun while she works.

Shit. I need to think things through before I open my damn mouth to make a promise. Especially when these two run the risk of directly contradicting each other. Keeping it professional while still keeping it fun? How do I factor in keeping it in my pants?

My phone buzzes twice with back-to-back texts. I read the first one.

Peyton: Made it home safe! Thanks for showing me the hotel. xo

My dick jerks against my zipper in response.

Dear God. Tonight has been torture. The second text is far more professional.

> Peyton: When would you like to meet next to discuss our budgeting and potential earnings for my product release?

A little work, a little play. This woman is wild. But it's a balance I may be able to maintain, as long as I keep it way more focused on the work part. Which means not replying to that first text.

I respond with an offer to meet tomorrow, and since I'm suggesting working on a weekend, I tell her to meet me at Scoops downtown.

Because what says *fun and professional* more than discussing finances over ice cream?

CHAPTER TWELVE

Peyton

When was the last time I was asked out for ice cream?

I'm not entirely sure, but if I were to guess, I'd probably say freshman year of high school. Somewhere around turning eighteen, we transitioned from ice cream to coffee dates and never went back. So when I get a text from Josh asking if I want to hammer out details of the deal over chocolate-dipped cones, I double- and triple-read the text to make sure I'm not imagining things.

After my fourth and final read, my thumbs fly across my phone screen to respond with an enthusiastic *yes!*

A business meeting over ice cream—what a concept. It's refreshing, both literally and figuratively. I guess CEO Josh Hanson has a playful side after all. He did mention he eats loads of ice cream on the weekend, though, so that explains the choice of locale.

After grabbing my keys, I shoot Gram a quick text letting her know I'm off to a meeting with Josh and won't be by the senior center until later. She responds almost instantly with an onslaught of heart and tongue emojis. *Sheesh. Way to be discreet, Gram.*

On my way out the door, the foyer mirror reminds me that my slouchy pink sweater and jeans don't exactly scream "professional." Should I throw on a pencil skirt and a button-down, or something else instead? I decide against it, slipping into my brown booties and then locking the door behind me. I'm guessing this ice cream shop won't have much of a dress code.

When I arrive at Scoops, Josh is already waiting outside, leaning against the building. He looks like a popular kid leaning against the lockers. This really is high school all over again. He's got on a black T-shirt underneath an Army-green jacket and dark-wash jeans, proving that he's just as drop-dead gorgeous in casual clothes as he is in a suit. I'm glad I nixed the pencil-skirt idea.

"Welcome to Scoops," Josh says with a warm smile. "I'm so excited for you to try this place."

I can hardly get out a *hello* before he's leading me up the steps and through the door. *Excited* might be a bit of an understatement.

A bell rings as the door swings open, welcoming us into the warm, sugary air. The storefront is filled with the sweet scent of fresh-baked waffle cones. The space is small and lit with warm, yellow light, with bright blue tables scattered throughout, and black-and-white photos framed on the walls. It's old school and charming . . . no wonder Josh loves it.

The moderate line to the counter consists mostly of parents and kids. A few high school couples are scattered here and there, confirming my theory on the switch to coffee that comes with maturity. Josh peels off his jacket and tosses it over the back of a chair, claiming a table for us before we hop in line.

As I size up the menu, Josh leans in, offering his recommendation. "No pressure, but they do have the best chocolate-dipped cone I've ever had," he whispers, as though excellent ice cream is somehow a secret. His lips graze my ear, spreading a buzz of pleasure across my skin.

"High praise from a professional ice-cream taster like yourself," I say, chuckling.

"Hey, what can I say? Everyone has their vices. And I'm not much of a coffee drinker, so ice cream it is."

How fitting that someone as sweet as Josh would have such a sweet tooth.

When we reach the front of the line, the woman at the register beams in recognition. "Chocolate-dipped cone, Josh?" she asks in a bubbly voice, already reaching for her scoop.

"Just like always, Connie." Josh laughs, then adds, "And whatever this lovely lady is getting as well."

"Make it two dipped cones, please," I say proudly, which gets a smile out of both Connie and Josh.

"Great taste, this one," Connie says, waggling her eyebrows at Josh as she reaches for a second cone.

When she rings us up, I mean to check if Josh

uses his personal or corporate card—is he paying for me as a date or as a business partner? But he moves too quickly for me to get a good look. Either way, I thank him for paying as we make our way to our table. The second we settle into our seats, Josh goes into full business mode.

"Okay, so I don't want to completely overwhelm you with financial stuff, so stop me if you've heard enough about profit margins. Sound good?"

I nod, appreciating the image of a man holding an ice cream cone telling me about profit margins. It's immediately clear that we're not going to discuss what happened in the hotel coat closet, which is a bit of a relief. I'm not sure I have a good explanation for what happened, and if we don't put in some hours on this Wish Upon a Gift deal, it's never going to turn out.

Josh launches into his spiel on his company's reimbursement model, and unlike his tour of the hotel, I'm able to pay attention to what he's saying this time. I pull my planner from my bag and flip to the notes section, writing down percentages as he throws them at me. I'm impressed by the cut of sales that the company offers its business partners.

When he pauses, I look up from my notes to find Josh licking the ice cream dripping down the side of the cone. Suddenly, my professionalism has flown out the window.

God, I want him to lick me like that. Cover me in chocolate and lick away.

"Sorry." Josh laughs when he catches me staring. "I don't want to waste any. Like I said, everybody has their vices, right?"

I nod, echoing the statement back to him in an almost breathy tone. "Everybody has their vices." I'm just worried he might be mine.

"Anyway, back to the reimbursement model."

We both snap out of our daze and back into business mode, finishing off both our discussions and our dipped cones. The notes section of my planner is overflowing with information, but we're definitely a step closer to getting my boxes on store shelves.

Josh pulls a napkin from the dispenser in the middle of the table. "Now that the boring stuff is out of the way, I have to ask."

My throat clamps up. *Shit.* We're gonna talk about that hot make-out sesh in the coat closet after all, aren't we?

"Have to ask what?" I ask meekly as Josh

swipes the napkin across his lips, then balls it up in his fist.

"Was I right?"

Confused, I blink at Josh. "Right about what?"

He smiles coyly, leaning into the table. "Was that the best chocolate-dipped cone you've ever had, or what?"

CHAPTER THIRTEEN

Peyton

There are many words I would use to describe my grandmother. She's nurturing, funny, and smart. She's a long-standing bingo champion and the life of the party at the senior center. She's my best friend. But if there's one thing that Gram definitely is not, it's subtle.

Since the moment Josh shook Gram's hand at the hotel event, she's been a woman obsessed. We can't get through a meal or a commercial break without her bringing him up, every conversation revolving around him as though he were my own personal Prince Charming.

Tonight's dinner conversation is no exception.

Leave it to Gram to be talking about today's episode of *Wheel of Fortune* and somehow manage to remind me how handsome Josh looks in a tux. As if I could forget.

"Speaking of Josh, you never told me about that meeting you and he had the other day." Her voice is light and airy, but her innocent tone isn't fooling me for a second.

"I've already told you about it twice, Gram." I lift my bowl to my lips and drink the last of the broth. Soup again. Tonight, it's alphabet. Nothing but gourmet cooking from Chef Peyton.

"Silly me, the old memory must be fading." Gram knocks on her head with her knuckles and clucks her tongue, making a hollow sound. "Won't you tell me one more time?"

I give Gram the most dramatic eye roll I can manage. "I'm not telling this story again," I say, feigning an annoyed pout.

Truthfully, I don't mind that she wants to talk about him so much. He's kind of my favorite subject to think about right now too. I'm just worried I'll slip up and mention a detail that I'd prefer my grandmother not know. Example A: the sexy selfie that started this mess in the first place. Or Exhibit

B: the hottest make-out session of my life at the hotel.

But the woman has been starved for any sort of romantic gossip from me for years, so who could blame her for hanging on to the little bit she's finally getting? If she knew what happened in the coat closet, I'd never hear the end of it. Gasoline, meet fire.

"All done with that?" I ask, pivoting the conversation with a nod toward Gram's nearly empty soup bowl. She smiles and gently pushes it across the table to me, a shit-eating grin on her face as she glances down at the almost-empty bowl.

There are four tiny noodle letters left: J-O-S-H.

You've got to be kidding me. I give her a pointed stare, and she merely grins wider. The little rat.

After rinsing out the bowls and loading them into the dishwasher, I reach for my phone and fire off a text to the group chat with the girls.

Peyton: Can you guys meet at Speakeasy in 15?

Their response is almost immediate—two thumbs-up emojis from each of them. Thank God.

I need advice from someone who doesn't qualify for a senior discount.

It's been a while since I've been the one calling for an emergency happy hour. Ever since Libby and Sabrina got engaged, last-minute Speakeasy trips have been nearly a weekly occurrence. There's no better way to discuss the minutiae of wedding planning than over a round of martinis. Although I'm perpetually single, my bridesmaid résumé is impressive enough that I've become somewhat of a guru of rational, levelheaded wedding advice.

But tonight, I'm the one who needs guidance. And lots of it. So when I take my usual seat at our table across from Sabrina and Libby, I'm ready to spill. All I have to do is mention Josh's name, and they're all ears.

"I don't know what to do, guys." I sigh, propping my chin in my hands. "He's so sweet. Beyond sweet. And funny. And smart. But maybe he's just that way with all of his potential business partners, you know?"

Sabrina gives me a doubtful look. "Do you think he's making out with all of his potential business partners? Not likely, girl. I think you should go for it. You're single. He's hot. Why not ask him out on an actual date?"

I let out a frustrated groan. "You sound like Gram. I swear, if she had things her way, Josh and I would be halfway down the aisle by now."

"Yay! Then we could all plan our weddings together!" Libby squeals and claps her hands, which Sabrina puts a stop to before I even have a chance to roll my eyes.

"Slow your roll, Libby. They're not even dating. They're just working together, remember?"

"Pretty tough to get much work done from inside a coat closet," Libby mutters under her breath before she takes a sip of wine. Tonight, we've opted to split a bottle, but by the end of the evening, I won't be surprised if we finish off a second one.

"Once," I remind Libby. "We've only kissed once."

Although I'm not sure it's fair to even call that a kiss. If it is, every other man on the planet is doing it wrong. It was hot and passionate, and oh my God, sexy. The little growly sound he made in his throat when I sucked on his tongue? The funny way he teased me when I begged him to stop being such a good kisser? And don't even get me started on that orgasm. It's just so easy to be with him. He's fun and sexy.

"You've only kissed once *so far*," she says, wagging a finger at me. "And from what I remember of your text synopsis, it was more than a kiss. It sounded like it was pretty damn earth-shattering, Peyton. Maybe he's actually serious about you."

"Yeah, because you were trying to get serious with every guy who you made out with in college, right?" I tease.

Libby shrugs, twirling a strand of red hair around her index finger. "No comment."

"All I'm saying is he very well could be buttering me up to try to close this business deal. How am I supposed to tell?"

Both Sabrina and Libby tap their manicured fingernails on their wineglasses as they sip, mulling it over.

"Wait! I've got it!" Sabrina pounds her empty glass on the table to punctuate her epiphany. "When he bought you ice cream, did he pay with his personal card or his corporate card?"

I try and fail to suppress a snicker. Sometimes, I swear she and I share a brain. "Great thought, but I already tried that. He moved too quickly for me to get a good look."

"Well, what if you just flat-out asked him?" Libby says. "Just ask if the whole coat-closet fiasco was a one-time deal." She shimmies her shoulders suggestively, and I cough to keep my wine from going down the wrong pipe.

"And run the risk of totally embarrassing myself if he says it was a fluke? No thanks."

"I say you just go for it," Sabrina says matter-of-factly, refilling her empty glass. "If you're worried about embarrassment, need I remind you that this dude literally sent you a dick pic out of the clear blue? There's nothing you can do that's half as embarrassing as that."

I nod, taking a good, long sip, regretting that I ever told them about that photo. "Okay, you're definitely right about that."

"I'm right about *everything*." Sabrina laughs as she waves down the bartender, gesturing for another bottle of white zinfandel.

I knew it would be a double-bottle night. As our server uncorks the bottle, the conversation shifts to wedding seating charts, an area I have absolutely zero expertise in.

My feigned interest only lasts so long before I tune out, letting my attention wander to my schedule for the upcoming week. I'm booked solid with meetings, something I'll have to get used to if this deal goes through smoothly. If things go as planned, my boxes will be in stores in a matter of weeks. If I think I have zero free time right now, it's about to sink into the negative.

What are the chances of me scrounging up enough free time to pursue things with Josh? Assuming he really is interested and wants more than a one-and-done hookup and isn't some playboy . . .

"Hello? Peyton? Are you there?" Libby yanks at my sleeve, jolting me out of my daze.

"Yeah, yeah, I'm here," I lie, putting on my best *I'm so interested in the details of your wedding* face.

But in my mind, I'm somewhere else entirely—sitting in a cozy ice cream shop or stumbling into a hotel coat closet. It's almost crazy how easily I can picture Josh and me juggling both a business and a personal relationship.

That is, if he's even capable of a relationship. I'm unsure of the overlap on guys who send dirty pictures to random women and guys who are looking for anything serious, but I'm hoping and praying that it's a Venn diagram with Josh Hanson sitting right in the middle.

CHAPTER FOURTEEN

Peyton

"**G**ram? Are you up?"

Apart from the low rumbles of the brewing storm, the house is uncharacteristically quiet tonight. Usually, when I return from a night out with Sabrina and Libby, I'm greeted by one of two things—Gram's rapid-fire questions about my evening, or the sound of her snoring from the couch. But tonight? Nada.

I toss my keys onto the kitchen table, and the metallic sound echoes throughout the house. Where the hell is she?

I check the clock on the stove—it's nine thirty. We haven't even reached the time of night where the infomercials start playing yet, which is when

Gram typically calls it a night. It's not like her to opt for an early bedtime, especially on a weekend. Maybe she caught a ride to the senior center and just forgot to text me.

"Gram? You home?" I try a second time, bounding up the stairs two at a time. Still no response.

My stomach bottoms out momentarily, but I wave off the panic as I head for Gram's door. She's probably just sleeping or online shopping or—

When I swing open her bedroom door, every nightmare I've ever had starts playing all at once. Gram is on the floor, as still as stone.

"GRAM!"

Hearing her name, she looks up at me with pitiful eyes, and I'm equal parts heartbroken and grateful. At least she's conscious.

"I fell," she whispers, grasping unsuccessfully for a grip on the side of the bed, then falling back down to her side with a light thud, no louder than the sound of a suitcase tipping over. No wonder I didn't hear her from downstairs.

I scramble to her side, taking her full weight against me as I help her to her feet. She winces and yelps when she tries to stand on her own, her small frame folding into my arms.

"I'm fine, I'm fine," she mutters through clenched teeth. "I just—ah, Jesus!" Her back cramps up and she recoils, one trembling hand gripping the small of her back as she swears under her breath. "These goddamned piece-of-shit shoes have no grip to 'em."

I can't help my slight smile at her potty mouth. After some awkward shifting and plenty of groans of pain from Gram, I manage to settle her onto the bed in a half-fetal position.

"I'm calling an ambulance." I reach for my back pocket to grab my phone, but even in her fragile state, Gram musters a bark of resistance.

"No way, José. Do you know how much a ride in one of those things costs? I'll be fine."

"You're not fine, Gram. And I can't take care of you all on my own. You need to see a doctor."

"But we can't afford it!" she whines. "Just get me an ice pack."

Only Gram would give me lip when she can't even stand upright.

"The only thing I'm getting you is medical attention," I tell her sternly. "And that's the last I want to hear on the subject."

I thumb in my phone password, considering my options. I could just call 911, despite Gram's wishes. Or Libby or Sabrina. They went straight home after Speakeasy, and I know either of them would be here in an instant to help out however they could. But for reasons beyond my understanding, my fingers fly across my phone, frantically searching for Josh's contact and pressing **CALL**.

"Hello, this is Josh." He sounds wide awake and alert, and I'm immediately certain that I made the right call.

"I need your help. It's Gram. She fell." I speak in short, panicky sentences.

"Text me your address. I'm leaving now." There's a muffled rustling sound, probably him putting on his coat, then a few seconds later, the squeak of a door swinging open into the rain, which is falling steadily now. I guess he's really coming. "Does she need an ambulance?"

I gnaw on my lower lip, giving Gram a sideways glance. She looks so defeated, trembling on the bed. "She doesn't want me to call one. She says it's too expensive."

Josh doesn't miss a beat. "Tell her my company insurance will cover it. I'll call it for you. I'm gonna hang up so you can send me your address, okay?"

"Okay," I squeak back. "Hanging up now. See you soon." I end the call and share my location with Josh. That'll be faster than having him type the address into his GPS.

"You're not calling a damn ambulance, are you?" Gram mumbles through a groan of pain.

"No, *I* am not. Josh is. He said the company insurance will cover it."

I may only have a view of half of Gram's face, but I can tell the smile stretching across her face must be ear to ear. Only she would get excited about Josh stuff at a time like this. I could feign annoyance about it, but I don't have the energy to. Instead, I approach the bed, taking Gram's soft hand and running my thumb across the bluish veins on the back of it. I'm so thankful for her. So thankful she's alive.

"That Josh is a good guy," she whispers, giving my hand the tiniest, gentlest squeeze. "A really, really good guy."

I don't even have a response to that, because in my heart, I think I already know how good he really is.

When the sirens approach, I run downstairs to welcome two ambulances' worth of EMTs, soaking wet with rain. I gesture toward the staircase, and without further instruction, they rush past me with swift precision, their black boots leaving wet prints on the carpet runner.

No niceties, no nothing. For them, this is routine, but for me, my own house suddenly seems foreign, like the set of a medical drama. Everything is blurry and unrecognizable.

I try to follow them up the stairs, but a paramedic keeps me downstairs, offering me a forced smile as she reminds me they'll need to keep the path clear to carry Gram down on the gurney. I want to shriek, to tell her that Gram would want me to be up there, but instead, I swallow my panic and nod. *She's in good hands*, I remind myself, but that doesn't stop my heart rate from climbing faster than those EMTs took the stairs.

Moments later, Josh arrives, both his leather jacket and the fitted gray tee underneath it soaked through with rain. Although he's never been in my house before, something about having him here is comforting, familiar, like slipping into an old, worn-in sweater.

He looks at me, saying nothing, because his eyes tell me everything I need to know. When he opens his arms, I give in, falling into his embrace as the tension in my shoulders releases for the first time since I came home. A sob escapes me, and the tears I've been holding back spill onto his shoulder.

"Shh, you're okay," he whispers, smoothing my hair with his hand as I bury my face in his chest.

The thought occurs to me that this isn't the type of thing someone does for a potential business partner, but I dismiss it, focusing instead on the smell of the storm on his skin. It's cool and relaxing, and I'm able to breathe a bit more steadily when the EMTs reappear on the stairs, carrying Gram down on the stretcher.

"This is ridiculous," she yells over the chaos. "Do I hear you crying, Peyton? Knock that shit off. I'm gonna be fine."

One of the medics looks at Gram like she's out of her mind, but I laugh, using the side of my hand to wipe away the evidence of my tears. Leave it to Gram to give me sass as she's carried out the door by the paramedics.

The flashing red lights are blurred by the rain, but the sirens are just as loud as ever. Off she goes.

As I watch the lights disappear into the storm, I feel a hand on my shoulder—it's the same paramedic with the forced smile from earlier.

"From what we can tell, your grandmother is going to be just fine," she says gently, reassuring me. "The doctor will want to examine her just to make sure there's no head injury or broken bones. It's nothing we'd keep her overnight for. Maybe your boyfriend can drive you to the hospital so you'll all have a ride home tonight."

I freeze, my mouth falling open as I stutter, grasping for words to correct her on her assumption. To my surprise, Josh is unfazed. He reaches out and shakes the paramedic's hand, returning her forced smile with a genuine one.

"Sounds perfect. Thank you for all your help. We'll follow your ambulance."

The last of the medics pile into the second ambulance and they peel off down the road, with Josh and me right behind them in his car. He holds my hand as he drives, steering with the heel of his left hand. He keeps his attention glued to the road, and I try to do the same, but every part of me desperately wants to lean over the console and kiss him, to pour all my gratitude from my mouth to his.

"I owe you one," I finally whisper as Josh turns the car into the hospital parking lot. It's not how I want to express my thanks, but it'll do for now.

"You don't owe me anything, Peyton."

I shake my head, a shaky sigh escaping my lips. "I don't know what we would've done if your insurance didn't cover the ambulance."

One corner of Josh's mouth twitches into the cutest half smile as he shifts the car into park. "Insurance doesn't cover it, actually. I knew if I told you otherwise, you wouldn't have agreed," he says, combing his fingers through his wet hair. "But I've got it. Don't worry about it. I've got you."

As he turns his head, pointing those sharp blue eyes and that adorable smile my way, a flutter builds in my chest, his words echoing in my head.

He's got me.

CHAPTER FIFTEEN

Peyton

"All right, Gram, I think that's about the last of it."

This has to be the fourth or fifth basket of Gram's makeup and hair products that I've lugged downstairs from her bathroom. I always knew my grandmother was much hipper than me, but who knew she'd have multiple contouring kits?

After setting the basket down next to the others, I scan the living room, now full of all of Gram's belongings, searching for anything we might have missed.

One end table was easily converted into a bedside table, and the linen closet in the hall is now filled with all her clothes. Josh, being the angel he is, has been here helping out since first thing this morning. And thank the Lord for him, because it would have been a complete disaster if I tried to get Gram's bed down the stairs by myself. Even with the extra help, we still had to face the obstacle of Gram trying to block the staircase with her walker, insisting that she could just sleep on the couch. Like her back isn't messed up enough.

"Looks like we're all set," I say, surveying our surroundings. "You should be entirely able to function on the first floor only."

"Thank you so much, you two. Although I still think I could've made it up and down the stairs once a day to go to bed." Gram looks at Josh, her eyes filled with hope that he'll side with her, but he just chuckles and shakes his head, lifting his hands in surrender.

"I'm staying out of that argument. I just want you to recover as fast as you can. So if there's anything else you need, just say the word."

Gram's mouth stretches open in a gaping yawn. "What I need right now is a nap, I think." She scoots across the carpet with her walker and lowers herself onto her bed, testing the springs with a few careful bounces. "And wouldn't you know it, I'm already in my new bedroom."

"We'll give you your privacy," I say, tilting my head toward the staircase. "I've got laundry to fold anyway. And, Josh, I'm sure you have a million and one more important things to be doing on a Saturday."

Josh scrunches his brow. "I don't have anything to rush off for. I'm more than happy to lend a hand with laundry, if you want."

Without even looking Gram's way, I can feel her look piercing through me, urging me to take him up on the offer. When I don't say anything right away, she lets out the biggest, most dramatic fake yawn I've ever heard.

"Yeah, I'm pooped. Peyton, you must be real tired too. A little help with laundry would probably go a long way."

I can barely hold back my eye roll. Apparently, even a minor back injury can't dethrone the queen of subtlety.

Don't get me wrong, I would love for Josh to stick around. Actually, I think I might want him to stay a little too much. When he showed up at the door this morning with a box of doughnuts and a positive attitude about the manual labor I had in store for him, I could have ripped the man's clothes off then and there. And I'm not going to pretend that I didn't get a level of enjoyment out of seeing him move furniture. The way his muscles rippled when he moved that bed sent a shock wave through my veins. And I'm fairly certain Gram noticed.

"It's up to you." I shrug, doing my best to play it cool as I switch off the lights in what is now Gram's bedroom.

With Josh close behind, I pad down the hall, my socks sliding on the hardwood all the way to the base of the stairs where my laundry basket of clean socks awaits. I scoop it up and rest it against my hip.

"Here, let me." Josh reaches to take the basket from me, but I swivel away, moving it out of his grasp.

"Let me carry this one thing. You've been hauling furniture around all day like a regular Hercules. I think I can handle one little laundry basket."

Josh's mouth twitches into a smirk, and my skin responds accordingly by flooding with goose bumps. "Fine, you're right," he says in surrender.

"Damn right I am." I smile. Those are some terms I can agree on.

Josh follows me up the stairs and down the hall to my bedroom door, where I suddenly jolt to a stop.

I was planning on folding laundry in my room, but is it crossing a line to bring Josh in here? There's something that seems entirely unprofessional about bringing your business partner into the bedroom. Then again, beds haven't really been our thing so far. We're more of a hotel-closet type of couple.

No. Bad Peyton. We are not thinking about the hotel closet right now. And more importantly, we are not, under any circumstances, a couple.

"Are you leading the way or am I?" Josh asks with a tap on my shoulder. I guess I paused here a moment or two too long.

"Uh, yeah," I stammer, searching the back corners of my brain for an excuse. "I'm fine. I couldn't remember if I turned the lights off for Gram. But I just remembered that I did."

Rolling my shoulders, I take the quietest deep breath I can and push open my bedroom door. I need to chill the hell out and stop making this out to be a bigger deal than it is. He's just here to help me out during a tough time. And the last time

I checked, *folding laundry* isn't exactly code for anything sexy. Unless sorting socks turns him on.

Josh sits on the bed next to me as I tip the laundry basket, causing an avalanche of socks to tumble onto my comforter.

"I think it's easier to sort them this way," I say, snagging two navy blue socks that I know are mine. "Thanks again for helping out so much today. It really means the world."

"My pleasure." Josh's gaze flits across the pile as he grabs a banana-yellow sock with a monkey-face pattern, then quickly finds its match. "These are fun."

"Gram's," I tell him, folding the navy socks together and tossing them back into the empty basket. "What can I say? She's a lot more fun than I am."

Interest sparks in Josh's eyes as he spots something in the pile. "I don't know about that." He smirks. "Because these look like a whole lot of fun to me."

From what I was sure was merely an innocent sock pile, Josh pulls a red satin thong, letting it hang off his fingers like a piece of evidence. I lunge to snatch it from his hands, but he yanks it back too quickly.

"Ah, so this is yours, I assume?"

The flush on my face is fire hot. Suddenly, the term "apples of my cheeks" makes perfect sense to me. I must be the color of a red delicious. Or more accurately, the color of the thong dangling from Josh's fingertips.

"Um, yeah. It's mine."

He runs a thumb along the silky fabric, a smug smile tugging at the corners of his mouth. "I knew it felt familiar."

My gut does a quadruple somersault as I process what he just said. *Holy shit.* Those are the underwear I wore to the hotel event. The pair he peeled aside before plunging his fingers into me and bringing me to the best orgasm of my life.

I bashfully tuck a loose strand of hair behind my ear, avoiding his gaze as my heart rate shoots through the roof. How am I supposed to respond to that?

When I muster the courage to look up, I find Josh with a crease of frustration on his forehead as he tries to fold the tiny scrap of red fabric. I snicker. He may be good with his hands, but I guess that doesn't include folding women's underthings.

"What?" Josh shoots me a defensive look, and I giggle again.

"Let's just say you did a little better with those panties the last time you had your hands on them."

My heart leaps into my throat. Um. What? Did those words really just come out of my mouth?

Josh seems as surprised as I am. His mouth falls open ever so slightly, and his eyes dance as they lock with mine. "Oh yeah?" He balls the silky red thong in his fist. "Well, I'd love a chance to do that again."

Sabrina and Libby's voices are practically screaming in my ears, telling me to go for it. This is it. This is my chance. Josh is sitting on my bed, less than a foot away from me, my panties in his fucking hands. And as loud as my best friends' voices are in my head, my own is even louder.

I know what I want. I want Josh.

I reach out and cup his stubbled jaw in my hand, enjoying the roughness on the pads of my fingers as I lean in. He meets me halfway, pressing his mouth against mine, taking my lower lip between his.

God, he tastes heavenly. Even better than I remembered.

Sliding his arms around my waist, he pulls me toward him till I'm settled in his lap, my legs wrapped around his waist.

Even through his jeans, I can feel his bulge stiffen beneath me as his hands make their way to the curve of my ass. A hungry moan builds in my throat, but I choke it back. It's dangerous enough to be making out with Gram sleeping downstairs. The last thing I want is to give her an unexpected wake-up call.

Just as I feel him getting fully hard, Josh lifts me off of him by my hips until I'm reclined against my pillows. I giggle as he pushes the mountain of socks off the bed and onto the floor.

"I'll deal with that later," he murmurs against my ear, causing every hair on my body to stand on end. "I've got something else to take care of right now."

With strong, nimble fingers, he tugs my leggings down to my ankles in one swift pull, taking my panties with them. His chest rumbles with a hum of approval, a hungry fire flickering in his eyes as he takes me in, wetting his lower lip.

"Goddamn." He groans, shaking his head. "Just as good as I imagined you'd look."

A flush of pink creeps down my cheeks and chest as he tosses my leggings and panties aside and kisses his way down my hips. It feels too good to be true, and definitely too good to be quiet.

A needy moan escapes my lips. "Fuck, Josh."

He looks up at me with hooded blue eyes, pressing one finger against his lips. "Let's not wake anyone up," he teases, then leans over to nip at the inside of my thigh.

My whole body shudders as his nipping turns to gentle kisses planted everywhere but where I want them. He slides his tongue along my thigh, so close to my center, and I let out a needy whimper, lifting my hips closer to his mouth.

"You're so perfect," he whispers against me.

Then, oh so slowly, he parts me with his tongue, getting his first taste. I can't help but gasp.

"Mmm." He smiles. "You taste amazing, angel."

His eyes flicker, their usual sapphire hue deepening to a stormy, sultry blue. And with that, he's gone, a man laser focused on his mission. His tongue runs expertly along me, lapping up every bit of wetness he can get his mouth on as my back arches into him.

I shudder and buck as he explores me, finding my most sensitive places and lingering there, holding me right at the edge. When he sucks on my clit, I'm done for. My thighs quake as I bite hard on my lower lip, trying to hold in my moans as he flicks his tongue one last time. Then everything within me releases, his name falling off my lips in a constricted sigh as I come undone.

Holy shit. This man may be good with his hands, but with his mouth, he's next-level extraordinary.

Planting one last gentle kiss on my hip, Josh rejoins me on the top half of the bed, pulling me into the crook of his arm where I can cuddle and catch my breath. The silence between us is warm and comforting, a moment of peace between what just happened between us and the inevitable: talking about it.

"So . . ." Josh finally breaks the silence, and the word lingers between us as he toys with a lock of my hair.

"So." I grin up at him, my lips quirked. "That

was . . . unexpected."

He shrugs. "What can I say? You're a little bit addictive, Miss Richards. I had to get a taste."

Maybe it's the post-orgasm adrenaline, or maybe it's the low, husky rumble of his voice, but every inch of me wants to give him a lot more than a taste. I want Josh Hanson to make a four-course meal out of me.

But before I can say a word, I hear Gram call my name from downstairs.

I bolt upright, and Josh does too. Quickly stepping into my panties and then my leggings, I watch with equal parts frustration and desire as Josh adjusts his erection and then opens the door.

"You'd better go check on her," he says.

"Are you okay?" I ask, moving toward the door.

"Of course." He nods. "I didn't do that because I expected something in return, Peyton. You don't owe me anything."

I nod once. A small warning bell rings in the back of my head somewhere as I begin to descend the stairs with Josh behind me. Of course I don't owe him anything. It would be wrong to trade sexual favors for help with my business. Which isn't what we're doing here. Is it?

I reach the bottom of the stairs in time to see Gram trying to heave herself up from the bed. "Damn walker's not close enough to the bed," she says, reaching for it.

"Here, let me." I move it closer to her bed where she can grip the handles to help her stand up.

"I didn't mean to bother you," she says, frowning. "But I really wanted one of those chocolate mint cookies we bought from the little girl next door."

I grin at her. "Oh, trust me, I get it. Those things are heavenly."

Gram toddles off to the kitchen, and I can feel Josh's gaze on me. When I turn around, he's standing by the front door, holding his coat.

I join him by the door. "Heading out?"

His chest inflates as he takes in a long, slow breath. "Yeah. I think I should probably go."

I'm not sure why, but it feels like something has shifted between us in the last few minutes. And I don't just mean Gram's untimely interruption. It feels like we're miles away from the playful banter we just shared about him finding my thong, and

I can only assume it's because he's thinking the same thing I am.

That it's probably not a good idea to keep doing this as long as we're still working together. It's too dangerous.

"Are you sure you have to go?" I ask.

"I probably should." He sighs, giving me a re-assuring squeeze.

"Because of work stuff?"

He swallows and places one hand loosely against my waist, letting it linger there—like he's not sure he wants to release me, but he's also not sure he can claim me. "I'm not thrilled about it either. But if your launch is going to be success-ful, we need to pump the brakes a bit here. I can't even think about work when I'm around you. Which would be the greatest thing of all time if we weren't, you know, working together. I don't want this to stand in the way of your business succeed-ing."

"You're right." I hate to admit it, although it doesn't stop me from snuggling up to him a little tighter. I don't want to let go just yet.

He gives me one last hug, and then calls out a good-bye to Gram.

CHAPTER SIXTEEN

Josh

If you're looking for the quickest way to feel like the world's biggest prick, here's my advice: take a girl away from her recently hospitalized grandmother and drag her on a business trip upstate.

Insta-douchebag. It works like a charm. Trust me, I know from experience.

I've offered Peyton a hundred different options that would allow her to stay home with Gram as she recovers from her fall. We can video conference her into our meetings, or even reschedule the trip altogether.

But Peyton insists on going, saying that she won't let anything stand in the way of her pitching her subscription boxes to our wine-country store managers. That woman is unstoppable. It's a major turn-on. And since she insists that Gram will be fine without her, I relent.

In an effort to make myself look like slightly less of an asshole, I offer to drive Peyton to the airport to save her on gas and parking. I'm thrilled when she takes me up on it. It's the least I can do to make this last-minute trip a little easier on her.

Plus, I like the idea of a little one-on-one time with Peyton before we spend the whole weekend acting professional in front of Brody and Toby. Emphasis on *acting*. I deserve an Academy Award for pretending I'm not instantly rock hard every time those brilliant blue eyes look my way.

"How is Gram? You're totally sure she's okay for the weekend?"

I've been genuinely worried about Peyton's feisty grandmother ever since she fell last week. Peyton has kept me as apprised as a coworker needs to be. Maybe a bit more, since I told her the ambulance is going on my insurance. Maybe she doesn't realize that my concern for her and Gram runs much deeper than our professional relationship. I know what it's like to lose someone you love, and I've been wondering if Gram's age and health are weighing on Peyton's mind.

But Peyton nods, her thick brown ponytail bobbing along. She looks so damn cute and comfy in her oversized denim jacket and leggings. It's probably the only time this weekend I'll see her in anything other than pencil skirts and heels, and I'm torn as to which version of her is sexier.

"Gram will be totally fine. She's already recovering super well."

"That's good to hear. She's obviously a very strong woman."

Peyton nods again, and I wonder if she's trying to convince me or herself. "Plus, her boyfriend, Duncan from the senior center, volunteered to play nurse for the weekend."

I stifle a chuckle as I flip on my turn signal, veering toward the airport parking garages. Of course Gram has a senior-citizen love interest. I should have known. It figures that some dude over twice my age is getting more consistent action than I am.

And for the record, that won't be changing this weekend. It's going to be a serious test of willpower to keep my hands to myself with Peyton staying in the same hotel as me. There's so much riding on these pitches this weekend, and it wouldn't serve either of us well to be distracted. Which is why I took action ahead of time by booking us rooms on different floors, on opposite ends of the hotel. Might as well set myself up for success, right?

I guess Peyton really can read my thoughts, because just then, she stops nervously twirling her ponytail and asks the question that's on my mind. "So we're going to, um, behave ourselves this weekend, right?"

I nod firmly. "The second we step onto that plane, we're on a business trip. I want your product launch to run smoothly, so yes, it will be one hundred percent business. No shenanigans. I promise I'll behave myself this weekend." Then I give her a sideways glance. "Will you?"

"Yes, of course I will," she says, answering almost too quickly. "Nothing but my best behavior all weekend."

I have to wonder if she's talking to me or to herself. Either way, it doesn't matter. I'm just glad we're both on the same page. It's the only choice.

Parking is no problem in the enormous airport lot. Security, on the other hand, is an absolute beast and a half. Somehow, the famously slow TSA line is moving at a pace that would make a snail look like an Olympic track star. When we finally get to our gate and meet up with the guys, the sigh of relief that comes out of Brody is almost loud enough to drown out the sound of planes taking off.

"Holy fuck, I thought you were going to miss the flight."

Toby clears his throat and tilts his head toward Peyton. "Language, Brody!"

"Oh. I mean holy crap," Brody says. "I mean holy . . . sorry, pardon my French, Peyton."

Peyton snickers, waving off Brody's apology. "I don't give a shit."

That gets a collective laugh from the group and takes the tension out of our shoulders, thank God. We don't need to bring any extra anxiety into what's already going to be a stressful trip. And not to make it a competition, but it's going to be a little extra stressful for the guy trying to keep his libido on lockdown.

"It's nice to finally meet you," Brody says to Peyton, extending his hand.

I forgot that they haven't actually met in person, only via phone call.

As we line up to board the plane, I flip the switch in my head to go into full business mode. No more scoping out Peyton's curves in my peripheral vision, or wondering if I could get her off through those leggings. I need to use this hour-and-a-half flight to check my sex drive at the gate and focus on what's ahead of me.

Unfortunately, what's ahead of me is my seat on the plane. And who is seated right next to me? None other than the world's sexiest travel companion.

Damn. I'm not sure if that's luck or some type of cosmic punishment.

I help Peyton stow her bright pink carry-on suitcase in the overhead bin, and she shimmies into the window seat.

Don't look at her ass, dude. Don't look at her ass.

Shit. I looked at her ass.

I slide into my own seat and clear my throat. As I focus on fastening my seat belt, I can't help but notice that Peyton looks slightly nervous.

"You okay?" I ask, gazing at her with concern.

She presses her lips into a line and fumbles with

her seat-belt latch. "This is probably a bad time to tell you, but I hate flying."

I take the seat belt from her trembling hands and fasten it, tightening the belt around her trim hips. "Which part bothers you? The takeoff? The landing?"

She smiles. "Um, all of it. The claustrophobic feeling of being locked in this flying deathtrap. The recycled air that makes me want to gag. The way my stomach jumps when we lift into the air."

I nod and press my hand over hers, which is gripping the armrest in a death-like grip. "Lucky for you I'm here, then. I have the perfect way to distract you from your fears."

"You do?" she asks, her wide eyes looking hopefully up at mine.

"I sure do. It's called a vodka tonic and a lively hand of rummy." I gesture for the flight attendant and pull a deck of cards out of my bag. "Are you game, or what?"

Peyton smiles. "My hero."

"The same room as usual, Mr. Hanson?"

With the number of trips I've made upstate, both for work and family, I'm damn near a regular at this hotel. I'm not sure if I'm proud or embarrassed that the front-desk ladies and I know each other by name.

"Same as usual, Pam. Thank you." I shoot her a grateful smile as I accept my keycard.

The team agreed to take a quick breather at the hotel before heading out for a working dinner. And after that flight, trying to share the armrest with Peyton while simultaneously fighting against the pressure building behind my zipper, I'm going to need a cold shower before I do anything work-related. Hopefully it will help get me in the right head space.

When I hit the elevator call button, I quickly realize that plan is going out the door. The elevator dings and slides open to reveal a very worried-looking Peyton, gnawing on her lower lip. She was the first one to check in and ventured off to her room a few minutes ago.

"Oh! Hi, again!" Her blue eyes widen as they lock with mine.

"Hi, yourself. Is everything okay?"

I move out of the way to let her off the elevator, but she doesn't move an inch. She just keeps biting that lower lip in a way that, frankly, I've been dying to do again since the second we stepped out of that coat closet two weeks ago.

"Um, actually, no. It's not really okay." She pauses, and I stick out an arm to keep the elevator door from closing. "I was on my way to the front desk because there's sort of a problem with my room." Her gaze is cast downward, as if the elevator carpet were suddenly the most interesting thing on the planet.

"Sort of a problem? What qualifies as *sort of* a problem?"

A nervous giggle slips from her lips. "Okay, not *sort of* a problem. A problem. But it's fine. I'm sure the woman at the desk can help me." She gestures toward the front desk, but cringes when she sees the huge line of people waiting to check in.

"They look pretty swamped. How about I just come check it out?"

I pause, trying to gauge Peyton's reaction. She knows as well as I do that the two of us shouldn't be alone together in a hotel room . . . with a bed, or a closet, or really any confined space away from prying eyes. But I'm not trying to pull anything. I'm just trying to help.

She must sense that, because moments later, we're both in the elevator, headed for her floor so I can scope out whatever *sort of problem* has Peyton so on edge. I'm assuming a questionable stain on the comforter or a broken TV that's stuck on the adult channel.

Nope. Much worse.

It was a massive understatement for Peyton to say that there's a *problem* with this room. There are problems. Multiple. As in maybe a few dozen. One window is stuck open, letting the chilly fall air blow in, and the whole place reeks of mold. And that's just my first impression. Between the unmade bed and the towels on the floor, this looks like a room that the cleaning crew forgot . . . for months.

"Holy shit, Peyton. I'm so sorry. I've stayed at this hotel dozens of times and never had an issue."

Scrubbing my hands through my hair, I assess the damage. Even if we get the hotel staff to clean up this dump, there's no immediate fix for the broken window or the mold issue.

I sit on hold with the front desk for ten minutes

before getting the info I was afraid of. As the huge line at the front desk suggested, they're all booked up for the night. They're willing to deep clean the place while we're at dinner, but switching Peyton's room isn't a possibility. I'm frustrated as fuck, but I still manage the politest *thank you* that I can before hanging up and pocketing my phone.

"Any luck?"

Peyton's voice is so sweet and hopeful that it nearly kills me to break the news that we're shit out of luck. I've got to do something to make this right. As much as I don't want to sleep in a cold, moldy room, it's looking like my best option.

I slide my keycard out of my front pocket and hold it out to Peyton. "Here. Take my room. Top floor, end of the hall. Room 1875."

She scrunches her brow at me and folds her arms over her chest. Damn, is she seriously going to be stubborn about this?

"What? No way."

"Come on, Peyton. I'm the one who booked this hotel. I can't let you sleep here in these conditions. Especially not since you'll be pitching to store managers all day tomorrow. I need you well rested."

I nod at the keycard again, urging her to take it. When she finally does, a soft, sweet smile spreads across her lips.

"Thank you," she whispers. "You're too good to me."

Her words hit me straight in the chest. Given the chance, I could be really, really good to her. But we agreed to be on our best behavior, and I'm going to do everything I can to stick to my word.

Dinner consists of plenty of business strategizing accompanied by plenty of wine. When in Rome, right? It's Peyton's first time to wine country, despite having lived in New York her whole life, and it would be a sin not to treat her to the fruits of the region.

If this trip were for pleasure instead of business, I'd be showing her all the best wineries, waiting for her reaction as the finest cabernet hit her tongue for the first time. Instead, the four of us are in a mid-level bistro across the street from the hotel, putting sauv blanc on Brody's corporate card while going over meeting notes. Not ideal, but I'll take what I can get.

"I'm not sure if I said thank you already," Peyton says softly, leaning in to speak just to me. "But what you did for me on the plane was really kind."

"It was nothing. I was happy to help." We played a couple of hands of cards and enjoyed a stiff cocktail together. It's hard to be stressed out when you're having fun.

"Well, I appreciated it. It was probably the most relaxed I've ever felt on a plane."

"Noted. On the way back, I can teach you spades. It's one of my favorite card games."

She laughs and swirls the wine in her glass. "That sounds like a plan."

"How are you feeling about tomorrow?" I ask, and glance at Brody and Toby. "Do you want to run through everything again?"

"That'd be great."

After a few glasses, a few entrées, and enough corporate talk to make any sane person's head explode, we all call it a night and head back to the hotel. We have a big day ahead of us tomorrow. Although I doubt I'll be sleeping too well in my chilly, moldy room. Looks like I'll be powered entirely by caffeine tomorrow, but it's worth it to be sure Peyton is safe and comfortable.

Brody and Toby join the group ahead of us stepping into the hotel elevator, leaving enough room for a toddler or two in the cramped space. Brody gives us an apologetic wave, mouthing *sorry* before the doors close and we have to wait for another open elevator.

I've still got most of a wine buzz going by the time we step into the next open elevator, so I'm sure it's the sauv blanc going to my head when I notice Peyton giving me a familiar look. It's the look I saw glistening in her eyes through the dark of the hotel coat closet last week. And it's certainly not the kind of look that says *I'm on my best behavior*. It's a look that screams *come and get a taste*.

But I've got to be imagining it? Right? So then why is she biting that lower lip, making me want nothing more than to come over there and bite it for her?

Fuck it. Brody and Toby are in their rooms for the night. And I've got liquid courage on my side. Why not test the waters?

The elevator stops at my floor and I look straight at Peyton, keeping my eyes locked with hers as the doors open, then shut. I don't get off. "Let me walk you to your room to make sure you get in safe."

She nods.

When we get off on her floor, I follow her down the hall, trying to keep my expectations in check. Just because we're attracted to each other, just because we've flirted and talked and laughed all day, it doesn't mean she's going to invite me into her room. Well, technically, my room.

When we reach her room, we stop in front of the door, and I wait while she fishes the keycard out of her purse and swipes it against the sensor by the doorknob. Then she pushes open the door but doesn't go inside. My heartbeat increases steadily.

"Are you coming in with me?" There's that hope in her voice again. It's so fucking cute.

"I don't know. Am I?"

It's an honest question. I know I'm breaking our agreement here, and I don't want to push this an inch further than she wants it to go. So, I'm following her lead, and it looks like she's leading me straight into her bed.

We hardly make it three steps into the hotel room before crashing into each other.

My mouth finds hers so naturally, sucking and

biting at her lower lip as her hands explore the muscles of my chest and shoulders. She tastes like wine and honey and autumn, just how I remember. It's my new favorite flavor. When her hands hit the button of my jeans, my inhale is so sharp that Peyton hesitates.

"Is this okay?" she asks, pulling back from our kiss.

"Shouldn't I be asking you that?" I can't help but smile. "I mean, there's not much here that you haven't already seen."

A wicked flame lights up Peyton's eyes. "Oh, I remember," she coos, wetting her lips. "But I've been dying to know if pictures do you justice."

Next thing I know, that gorgeous, honey mouth I was tasting moments ago is trailing kisses down my abs until her lips are pressed against the button of my jeans. She carefully pops the button open as she sinks to her knees, pulling my pants and boxers to the floor and freeing my erection.

She's quiet for a moment, sizing me up and admiring her prize. Well, she looks at it like it's a prize, but I'm the one who feels like the biggest goddamned winner in the world. I've never had a woman just admire me like this before, and it's making me harder by the second.

Finally, she breaks her silence with one little syllable. "Yep," she whispers as she runs her palm along my shaft. "Verified to be way better in person."

And without another word, she parts her lips and claims me.

Jesus fucking Christ. Her mouth feels like heaven.

"Fuck, Peyton. That's so good." I can hardly get the words out between groans. Damn, this girl is good. Better than good. Un-fucking-believable.

She looks up at me with those big blue eyes and I'm gone, totally lost in her.

I rock my hips in time with her rhythm and she takes me deeper, swallowing my whole length down her throat. Just as I feel myself building to a climax, she slows down and takes me out of her mouth to work me over with her tongue, tasting every inch, all the way to the sensitive tip.

A groan rumbles in my chest as I shudder against her tongue, and just when I don't think I can take another second, she takes me in her mouth again, sending me hurtling toward the edge.

"Fuck. Gonna come now."

I grip her ponytail in my fist, a last-ditch effort to hang on for another second, but it's no use. I moan and free-fall over the edge, pouring into her until I'm left drained and spent and awestruck.

"Holy shit, Peyton." I cup her chin in my hand as she smiles up at me. "You didn't have to do that."

"I know," she says mischievously as I help her to her feet. "But I wanted to."

Once my boxers and pants have been returned to their rightful place on my hips, I pull Peyton flush against me and press a gentle, thankful kiss against her mouth.

"I really, really appreciate it. You're amazing. Just know that normally I don't let a woman make me come until I've given her at least one solid orgasm."

Peyton laughs. "But you have given me at least one solid orgasm," she says, then kisses my cheek. "You just gave me mine a week in advance. And I have to admit you've inspired a few more in the privacy of my bedroom, compliments of my vibrator and that picture you sent me."

Damn, that's a sexy thought. "Then let me offer

you at least one more."

I grip her hips and pull her in closer for a kiss. It was meant to be a chaste kiss, a kiss to feel out where she wants to take things next, but before I know it, Peyton is the one deepening our connection. As her tongue slides against mine, her hips rock against my pelvis and my cock begins to harden again.

"You're too much," I murmur between kisses. I tug down her leggings that have taunted me all day and find her silky core is already wet for me.

Shit.

And now I'm fully hard again.

We haven't even made it to the bed. We're still standing at the edge of it, both of us half dressed.

I stroke my fingers over her, and Peyton moans. Somehow I know she's not going to last long, and I love the idea that it's *me* she's losing control for— that I'm the one who's going to be holding her tonight.

One thing at a time, Hanson.

First, I have a favor to return. Remembering all the things that drove her crazy the first time, I thumb her sensitive clit while sinking two fingers inside her.

She shudders and groans out my name.

Wrapping one arm securely around her waist, I walk us backward toward the bed.

"Where are we going?" she asks, breathless.

"Let's get you onto the bed where you can be more comfortable."

But rather than move onto the bed like I imagined, Peyton freezes, her leggings around her thighs. She inhales sharply, holding it for a moment like she's trying to decide on the best call. When she finally exhales, she shakes her head and tugs up her panties and leggings.

"God, I want that so bad, Josh. But I know where that leads. And we can't sleep together. We both know that."

Fucking hell. She's probably right. But that doesn't make me want her any less.

"I can't just leave you hanging," I say, meeting her eyes and touching her cheek softly.

She shakes her head. "You're not. It's my choice. Tomorrow is quite possibly the biggest day of my career. I don't want to lose focus."

She sounds pretty damn certain, and a hollow ache forms in my chest at the thought of not touching her again.

"Well," I say, "just know it's redeemable at any time. An IOU, if you will."

She laughs again, wrapping her arms around my waist. "Oh, I will. But for now, please tell me you'll sleep up here and not in that certifiable death trap downstairs?"

"Only if you're not going to make me sleep on the floor."

"I think the bed's big enough for us both. Don't you?"

As Peyton claims the bathroom to get ready for bed, I strip down to my boxers and find my usual spot on the left side of the mattress.

It's weird to think about all the nights I've spent alone in this same hotel room, this same hotel bed. I'm here at least once a month for either family or business, and I've never even had anyone else in the room with me. Hotel room 1875 has been my own personal space, my little bit of territory in a town so entirely different from New York City.

But when Peyton struts out of the bathroom,

makeup-free and sleepy-eyed in an oversized T-shirt, I feel so fucking lucky that she's going to be stealing my covers tonight.

CHAPTER SEVENTEEN

Peyton

It may have taken a few glasses of wine and a trip upstate, but Josh and I finally talked things out. Well, we did a little more than talk last night. But the point is, the night in the hotel coat closet is no longer a big question mark in my brain anymore. And now that I don't have to overanalyze every word out of his oh-so-delectable lips, I can prioritize the *business part of this business trip.*

At least, that's what I told myself last night.

After Josh agreed that we shouldn't take things any further, I brushed my teeth, washed my face, and fell asleep, promising myself that I'd start the next day with a fresh perspective. Yes, my crush on

Josh is one hundred percent reciprocated, but he's also one hundred percent my business partner, and it's a relief that we both agreed to put the romance stuff on the back burner.

But now, in our third and final meeting of the day, I'm not sure if things are better or worse than before. As Josh reviews the timeline for the Wish Upon a Gift collaboration to a conference table of investors, I hardly catch every fifth or sixth word out of his mouth. That gorgeous mouth. When Josh speaks, he commands the attention of everyone in the room. Except for me. Because I know where that mouth really shines.

Shit. That's the thing about the back burner—it still keeps things hot.

I hear the words "boutique personalization in a big-name store," which I know is the cue for Brody to take the baton and wrap things up. It's a pretty re-hearsed process after three nearly identical pitches today. Like clockwork, Josh gives Brody the floor and takes his seat, his knee just barely brushing my thigh as he does.

And . . . cue the goose bumps.

Sheesh, Peyton. It's just a knee. But it's *his* knee. And that song from elementary school science class, the one that helped us learn the bones of the body, starts playing in my head.

The knee bone's connected to the thigh bone. And between the thigh bones . . .

"Great work today, Peyton. Three pitches in a day can be a lot."

Heat floods my cheeks as I stand to shake Brody's hand. "Thanks," I manage to say, blinking my way out of my fantasy. "Third time's the charm, right?"

"I think you charmed them on all three." Josh shoots me a wink, and the heat in my cheeks moves south.

"Well, the product really sells itself," I say, shifting my attention to packing up my portfolio of samples. "But it seems like these investors were especially into how customizable the gifts can be. Don't you agree?"

Nothing like a little business talk to bring the hormones back from the ledge.

Deep breaths, Peyton.

The last of the investors file out of the room, and Toby, Brody, Josh, and I are right behind them, headed toward our two rental cars. We've got a few hours before we need to head to the airport, but Toby and Brody have plans to grab a drink with an old coworker, leaving Josh and me with an afternoon to ourselves. And since checkout was at noon, we have no hotel room to return to. Which I'm slightly relieved by.

Josh ditches his suit jacket and tie, tossing both in the back seat of the rental with our luggage. He looks so incredibly sexy in just a button-up, his chiseled pecs on display through the fitted fabric. Sadly, I don't get too much time to stare. He climbs into the car and I join him, although I have no idea where he's planning to take us. But then Josh turns out of the parking lot and takes off on the highway, heading in the direction of the airport. Maybe we're just going to kill time at the terminal.

"You really crushed it today, Peyton. We were all totally impressed. Brody wasn't just saying that."

"I'm flattered. But I don't think I would've been half as good without you guys having my back."

It's the truth. As wildly distracting as Josh was during these meetings, he was also incredibly encouraging. All the guys were. Brody, Toby, and Josh couldn't have been more supportive if they'd showed up at our meetings in cheerleader uniforms, shaking pom-poms as I pitched. I can't help but giggle at the thought.

"What's so funny?" Josh asks, shooting me a suspicious smile.

"Oh, nothing." A satisfied grin lifts my lips as I redirect my attention to the road. "Just a funny thought."

"Here's another funny thought," he says. "Since we have some time on our hands, want to pay a visit to some of the craziest kids I know?"

I scrunch my brow at him. "Um, further context needed, please."

"My cousin Claire lives pretty close to here. She's got four little ones, all under the age of six. They're rowdy, but I love them. When I'm up here for work, I like to try to swing by for a quick visit, but I don't want to drag you along if you don't want. I can drop you at the—"

I cut in, interrupting perhaps a little too enthusiastically. "I'd love to meet them. I mean, it'd be a great change of pace from all the thrilling supply-chain talk we've had today," I add, doing my best impersonation of a girl with any amount of chill.

"Sounds great." Josh beams at me as he takes

the next exit off the highway.

We're both lucky I'm in the passenger's seat. If he threw me a smile like that while I was behind the wheel, we would have majorly regretted not getting the extra insurance on the rental car.

Claire, who Josh tells me is a full-time mom with yet another baby on the way, and her husband, an eighty-hour-per-week engineer, live just a few minutes off the highway. We park in the driveway behind a big navy-blue van, and when we ring the doorbell, a series of bells chime in a light, twinkling melody. It's a perfect portrait of suburbia.

"Uncle Josh!"

The door flings open and three tiny humans come bounding outside, wrapping their arms around Josh's legs and tugging at his sleeves. Behind them stands a brunette with a little girl propped on her hip. I'm guessing by the baby bump that this is Claire. She has pale purple marks under her eyes, just like the ones Josh gets after a late night at the office. If he hadn't mentioned that she was his cousin, I would have assumed Claire and Josh were siblings.

"All right, all right, one at a time. I've got enough hugs for everyone." Josh laughs, hoisting up the smallest of the group, a dark-haired toddler in denim overalls. "Connor, this is Peyton. Can you say, 'Hi, Peyton'?"

"Hiii, Peytonn," the whole group sings in unison. Even the little one on Claire's hip joins in with a squeal of delight.

I smile and wave—two boys and two girls. I guess the new baby will be the tiebreaker.

"I'm sorry the house is a mess," Claire says, tucking a loose strand of hair back into her messy bun. "I mean, the house is always a mess. But it's a bit more so than usual. Connor just had his second birthday party a few days ago, right, Connor?"

Connor nods proudly, then buries his face into Josh's shirt.

My heart flutters a bit at the sight of Josh with a little one in his arms. For a second, I even find myself imagining what our kids would look like. My hormones really need a reality check.

"C'mon, guys. Let's go show Peyton the cool playset I got you." Josh sets Connor down, and all three kids immediately take off running. "Last one there is a rotten egg!"

"No running in the house!" Claire half laughs,

half shouts after her kids. She attempts a disapproving look at Josh, but it quickly turns into a smile. "So, am I the rotten egg this time, or are you?"

Josh nods at the door, indicating that Claire and I should go ahead. "I volunteer as rotten egg," he says with a laugh. "It's a tough job, but someone's gotta do it."

Claire leads us down the hall, giving me an abbreviated version of a tour before we step into the backyard. The sprawling grass and big, climbable trees are like something out of a dream to me. Having a yard—front or back—was never a possibility for someone like me who was raised in the city. Swing sets and makeshift kickball fields were reserved for public parks or, more commonly, movies about kids living in the suburbs.

The acre and a half behind Claire's house could have been pulled right from one of those movies. In the center of the yard is a play structure with four swings, one for each kid, and a giant twisty slide the color of a school bus.

"Uncle Josh is a rotten egg!" One of the girls giggles from her place on a swing, which causes an outbreak of giggling among the three of them.

Josh pretends to smell himself and pinches his

nose, fanning away an imaginary rotting smell. It's enough for Claire and me to join in on the laughter. As the kids take turns on the slide, Claire tells me the story behind the playset, how Josh bought it for the kids and took a whole weekend to come upstate and assemble it.

"My husband has been working overtime to make up for his upcoming paternity leave." Claire pats her belly with her free hand, acknowledging the little one cooking in there. "I'm so grateful that the kids have a great male role model around like Josh during this time."

Josh's gaze is cast downward, a slight smile on his lips as he unbuttons and rolls up the sleeves of his shirt. "I'm just doing what I can." This has to be the humblest I've seen him since we met.

When Claire ducks back inside to put the baby down for her nap, the three little ones start vying for their uncle Josh's attention.

"You don't have to come play. I know you're not exactly dressed for it." Josh nods toward my red sheath dress and black blazer.

I squint my eyes at him. *Is that a challenge?* After kicking off my black pumps, I take off running toward the playset. "Race ya there, rotten egg."

The next hour and a half is spent rotating between playground games. It's been a long time since I've pretended that the ground is lava, but the kids seem to like teaching a grown-up how to play. During a round of hide-and-seek where Josh is 'it,' I give my hiding spot away early just so we can seek together, exaggerating how stumped we are as we turn blind eyes to the kids' blatantly obvious hiding spots.

Josh is a natural with the kids, but I didn't expect to take to them so quickly myself. When we say our good-byes before heading to catch our flight, Connor grabs my leg, begging his new aunt Peyton to stay. My heart is filled with something I can't quite name.

"I've never seen the kids like that with someone new," Josh says on the drive to the airport. "They really liked you."

"I liked them too. If we're in the area for business again, do you think we could go back?"

"Of course. Whatever you want."

Whatever I want? I stare off into the rolling green hills of the wineries. What *do* I want? I want this deal to go off without a hitch. That would mean a guaranteed paycheck. A big one. It would mean a better life for Gram and me.

But I've never been the kind of woman to only want one thing. And this other thing I want, the most beautiful human being I've ever laid eyes on, is just ten inches away from me, the heel of his hand draped over the steering wheel, giving me the perfect view of his angular profile while he keeps his gaze glued to the road ahead.

And now I know he wants me too. Which just makes all these feelings harder to ignore.

CHAPTER EIGHTEEN

Peyton

I wake up to the rattling of the plane as its wheels touch down on the runway.

I can't believe I feel asleep. I never sleep on planes. But after Josh taught me his favorite card game, we shared a strong cocktail. I guess the combination of the alcohol and the swift relief I felt about the presentations being over were enough to send my body into total shutdown mode.

When the plane rolls to a gentle stop at the gate, I smile at how good I feel. Home sweet New York.

Well, technically, we never left New York, but the hour-and-a-half flight from upstate might as well be a return journey from Mars with how different upstate is from Manhattan. And that's coming from someone whose home just barely falls within the NYC zip code.

That reminds me, I need to text Gram and let her know we landed.

I grab my phone and switch it out of airplane mode, then fire off a quick text. I want her to know I'm safe on the ground, but more importantly, I want to make sure no disasters took place while I was gone.

She responds right away that she's fine, a message that she accompanies with an eye-rolling emoji and a prompt request for a ride to the senior center. I shoot back a slew of red hearts. Even though she insisted I go on this trip, I still feel like the world's worst granddaughter for skipping town just days after her fall.

"That's a lot of heart emojis," Josh says. "Talking to someone special?"

I press my phone against my chest in defense. "Are you reading over my shoulder?"

"It's hard not to," he says coyly. "You're lying on my lap."

I jolt upright, my eyes nearly bulging out of my

head. What the hell? How did I not notice I was practically snuggling with Josh?

"How long was I like that?" I sputter, making no effort to hide how flustered I am.

My head was inches away from his crotch, albeit through his dress pants, but still. What if he thinks I did that on purpose as an excuse to get more one-on-one time with the appendage that got me hooked on him in the first place? Embarrassment floods my cheeks, but Josh doesn't seem to be bothered.

"Not that long," he says with a quick shrug. "Those kids must have really done a number on you." He unbuckles his seat belt and stands to pull both our bags from the overhead compartment. "No big deal. It was a short flight. And I didn't want to wake you. You looked too comfortable."

I breathe a shaky sigh of relief. Comfortable. That's exactly the right word to describe how I feel about Josh.

When we first met and he quickly realized I was his dirty-pic recipient, things were awkward for only a minute or two before we found a rhythm between us, a rhythm we've maintained ever since. Even when I didn't know where we stood, I felt unsure, sometimes confused, but never uncomfortable or on edge. I don't know what it is about him, but when we're together, it seems natural, like everything is the way it's supposed to be.

Josh is a seasoned pro at navigating LaGuardia with all the flying he does for work, so I let him navigate our way off the plane and toward the nearest coffee stand. Coming out of a thirty-minute nap, I could certainly use the caffeine boost to get me through the rest of the evening. Josh puts in my usual order for a hazelnut latte; for himself, black coffee. He puts it on the corporate card, reminding me we're technically still traveling for work until we get home.

"Speaking of home, do you need a ride back?" Josh asks between sips of his coffee.

I have to physically bite my tongue to keep myself from piping up with a comment about the kind of *ride* I'm interested in.

Josh catches me fighting for a response and interrupts. "Before you tell me I don't have to, let me say it's not an entirely selfless offer. I'd love to swing by and say hi to Gram, especially since I'm the one who dragged her roommate away for the weekend."

I can hardly believe how thoughtful he is. Coming to the rescue the night Gram fell was already above and beyond what I could ever ask, but checking in on her afterward is downright sweet. I keep a tight-lipped smile as I take a long sip of my latte, letting the milky hazelnut taste chase away my sleepiness.

"A ride home would be great. Gram would love to see you before I take her to the senior center."

"Just don't fall asleep on me during this trip, okay?"

I lift my pinkie finger into the air. "Pinkie swear."

Josh winds his pinkie tight around mine, pulling his hand against his lips to seal the promise with a kiss. "I'll hold you to it."

God, I'd give anything to be that hand.

A shiver flickers through me as the memory of last night dances through my head, the way those plush lips of his felt against mine. Of the way he felt in my mouth. Before I put the brakes on everything, of course. *It was the right thing to do*, I tell myself.

The drive home is surprisingly quick, the traffic gods graciously opting in our favor for the evening. Before I can dig out my keys, Gram swings the door open, doing an awkward celebratory jig behind her walker.

"She's home! My favorite worrywart!" She manages to wrap me in a tight, one-armed hug while balancing herself on her walker.

God, I missed her. Even if it was just a couple of days.

A gasp escapes her when she notices that I brought company with me. "Josh, how sweet of you to stop by," she coos. "I haven't gotten to properly thank you for saving the day when I took my little tumble."

I roll my eyes at her choice of words. "Little tumble" doesn't quite describe the incident. At least the doctor finally got her to understand that she was a little unsteady now and that it was safer to rely on the use of a walker.

We make our way inside and I drop my bag in my room. When I come back downstairs, Josh and Gram are nestled into the couch, chatting up a storm.

"There's gotta be a way to repay you," she says. "We don't have much money, but there has to be something." She spots me on the staircase, and a flicker darts across her eyes, paired with a mischievous grin. "Or maybe Peyton here could, you know, do a *favor* of some kind for you."

"That's enough of that, Gram," I snap. This whole back-burner thing is difficult enough without my freaking grandmother nudging us toward each other. Little does she know my evening of favors last night was, unfortunately, our last. "Do you want that ride to the senior center?"

"I'd love a ride, sweetheart. But don't worry about picking me up. Duncan can bring me back home." While Josh is busy fishing his keys out of his pocket, Gram shoots me a wink.

"I can drive." Josh jingles his keys in the air.

I scrunch my brows at him. "Don't you want to head out?"

The corner of Josh's mouth quirks into a partial smile. "Nah. I've got nothing going on tonight." He directs his smile toward Gram before adding, "It's the least I can do after hijacking your granddaughter for the weekend."

Luckily, Gram spares me any further suggestive innuendos on our drive to the senior center. Instead, she chats our ears off about tonight's Pinnacle tournament, taking the liberty of explaining the game in precise detail to Josh. I'm not sure whether he's faking it or not, but he acts genuinely interested, which Gram loves.

It does my heart a lot of good that they get along so well. Even if Josh can't be more than my business partner, we still have to be in each other's lives. And with me comes Gram. We're sort of a package deal.

Once Gram has been dropped off into the arms of her senior-citizen boyfriend, I expect Josh to turn around the way we came to take me home. Instead, he catches me off guard with a proposition of plans for the evening.

"We're actually closer to my apartment than we are to your place," he says. "And, full disclosure, I'm starving. How does bringing a pizza back to my place sound?"

A giddy thrill dances along my nerves. How does it sound? It sounds like a date, that's how it sounds. But inviting me over for a night of pizza and canoodling on the couch certainly steps outside of what we agreed to less than twenty-four hours ago.

"Or would you rather I just take you home?"

Shit, I paused too long.

"No, no, that's not it." I chew my lip, searching for the right words. I quickly realize there are none. To hell with it. "Pizza sounds great."

The pizza joint Josh swears by is a quick ten-minute detour on our route back to his place. That's the beauty of living in New York City: you're never more than a stone's throw from a pizza place. The bonus of living on the outskirts of town? Actually having a place to park your car.

Josh's building has its own parking garage, a luxury I thought was reserved for the millionaires of the Upper East Side. Then again, Josh is a high-level executive at the top wine distributor in the country. I'm sure he's not hurting for money.

I insist on being the one to carry the pizza box, using the warm cardboard in my hands as a distraction from how unbelievably sexy Josh looks.

"Feel free to make yourself at home," he says with a turn of the key. But the apartment behind that door is nothing like any home I've been in before.

Walking into the foyer, I quickly realize I was right about the money thing. Josh's apartment is completely decked out in classy, modern furniture, all white. Not the kind you buy for your college dorm room—the kind you see in the sorts of catalogues where they don't even list the prices. If you have to ask, you can't afford it. The only exception? A brown leather couch with a white throw draped over the back. It's worn in, not new like everything else.

"What's the story on this?" I kick off my shoes and head for the couch, dragging my fingers along the back.

"Kinda sticks out, huh?" Josh chuckles. God, that laugh. Gritty but sweet, like honey in a whiskey glass. "There's actually a story."

"As I expected." I take a seat, sinking into the cushions as I reach for the white throw and drape it over my lap. "I'm all ears."

"It used to be in my parents' living room," he says, making his way to the kitchen and popping the cork on a bottle of red. "In high school, I practically lived on the thing. When I moved from the suburbs to the city, they let me take it. A little reminder of where I came from." He returns with a glass of wine in each hand. "Do you think it's an eyesore?"

I shake my head as I accept a glass from him. "I

think that's super sweet. A great way to remember your roots. And you definitely make it work in the space."

His smile is proud, if not a little hypnotizing. If he's trying to get me under his spell, it's working. "What can I say? When I know what I want, I always make it work."

I gulp down the lump in my throat. Somehow, I feel like he's not just talking about the couch, so I pivot the conversation to something a bit more practical and a lot less sexy. "Isn't it a little dangerous to drink red wine on a white carpet?"

Josh's eyes narrow to slits, a smile tugging at his lips as he closes the space between us. He's close enough to get me buzzing before I've even had a sip of wine.

He raises his glass, waiting for me to clink mine against it. "Isn't it a little dangerous for us to be alone together when we said we'd keep it professional?"

I freeze, my mouth hanging open ever so slightly. It's not until he taps the rim of his glass against mine that I'm able to speak.

"I, um, I actually meant to ask you about that." I swirl my wine in my glass, careful not to let any spill. "Because this feels like a—"

"Like a date?" He finishes my thought, bringing a flush to my cheeks that's probably as red as the wine.

"Kinda. Is it?" I whisper, hope building in the back of my throat.

"Well," Josh says, setting his glass on the table before shifting so his broad shoulders are square with mine. "I had every intention of making good on our deal to take the romantic stuff off the table for now."

I set my glass on the coaster next to his. "Have or had?" I ask meekly, hoping I know the answer.

"Had." His fingers brush across my cheek, tucking my hair behind my ear before his hand finds a gentle hold on the back of my neck. "But you're certainly not making it easy on me. Look at you, for God's sake. What am I supposed to do?"

"Kiss me," I say in a whisper, surprising myself.

And he does. Not a second later, Josh's lips crash into mine and we fall into our rhythm again, our tongues intertwining as he explores my mouth hungrily. He slides my blazer off, exposing my shoulders and collarbone for him to kiss and nip and tease. It's only moments before my dress meets the same fate, unzipped and slid off, a bolt of red against the white carpet.

I toss my head back, a stifled groan of pleasure falling from my mouth as Josh's tongue moves from my collarbone to the space between my breasts, his breath hot and wanting. My nipples harden beneath my black lacy bra, tight and hard and ready for him. Every inch of my skin begs for his touch, every hair standing on end, every gentle bite against my neck fueling the fire building for this man.

Pawing at his shirt, I pop open the buttons one by one before shoving it off his shoulders, then drag my nails down his back until I get a hum of pleasure out of him. God, I've wanted to hear that hum so desperately since the moment I slammed on the brakes last night.

I'm already panting in need by the time Josh pulls back.

"Are you sure about this?"

I almost laugh, but instead smile devilishly, reaching out and taking a handful of his hardness through his pants. He groans again as I tighten my grip, feeling him harden even more beneath my touch. "I need this."

"Where, baby?" he growls. "Show me where."

Pushing one thigh to either side of him, I straddle him, grinding against the solid ridge I can feel between my thighs. "Here."

He's fully erect now, and he releases a soft grunt when I rock against him again. I could ride him like this. Right here. Right now.

But Josh has something else in mind first. Lifting me by my hips, he pulls me off of him and onto the couch before his knees hit the plush white carpet. One twist of his fingers, and the fabric of my soaked panties is pulled to the side, his hot mouth against my wetness, breathing me in.

"You're so fucking wet, sweetheart."

He runs one finger along my wet flesh, his tongue chasing quickly behind it, and I shudder. As he touches my clit with his tongue, he eases two fingers into my tightness until I'm quivering around him.

"Here?" he asks, his mouth not straying from that bundle of nerves at my center. He curls his fingers inside me to indicate where he's referring to.

"Is this where you want me?"

"Y-yes," I stutter.

He's so talented, so focused when he goes after what he wants, and it's obvious right now that he wants me. I'm nearing climax already, but he's not going to let me have it yet. Rising to his feet, he shakes his head.

"Not here. Bedroom."

When he scoops me into his arms, I steady myself against his chest as he carries me down the hall. He nudges open his bedroom door to reveal another crisp white room with a queen-sized bed covered in the fluffiest white duvet. It looks familiar, but it's not until he sets me down on the bed and starts unbuckling his belt that it hits me.

I'm sitting on the backdrop of Josh's dirty photo. The first-impression pic that started it all.

As Josh unbuttons his pants, I watch in anticipation. My favorite picture is about to be recreated, and I can hardly wait.

CHAPTER NINETEEN

Josh

Since the first time I laid eyes on Peyton, I've wanted her in my bed, on top of my fluffy white comforter, not a scrap of clothing on her. I've pictured her like this more than I'd like to admit, her dark brown hair spilling over her bare shoulders, her blue eyes wide and wild with anticipation.

And now, here she is, exactly how I imagined her. But even in my head, it never looked quite this good.

Gripping the curve of her hips, I ease Peyton to the edge of the bed until her legs drape over the side, that tantalizing space between them about level with my thighs. Fuck, she's gorgeous. Like a damn painting, but better. There isn't a museum out there that can offer me anything as hot as Peyton's peachy skin against my white sheets, wet and ready for me.

She props herself up on her elbows to watch as I step out of my boxers, giving myself a few strokes for good measure. Not that I need them. She's got me totally hard just lying there, running her tongue across her lower lip. But she's so mind-blowingly gorgeous, and I've been waiting for what feels like forever to get my eyes on this view. Might as well soak it in while I can.

"Ready?" I ask, confirming what her eyes are telling me.

She nods, and I lean in to press a kiss to the soft skin of her neck, letting her scent wash over me. Autumn and honey, like always. I would bottle it, if I could.

She shudders against my breath as I let my lips linger on her neck, my erection pressed against her belly. I press the heel of my hand against the juncture of her thighs, then feel her back arch beneath me when I take it away. Teasing her shouldn't be this fun.

"God, yes," she begs on an exhale. It's the sexiest thing I've ever heard.

While I sheath myself with a condom from my bedside drawer, Peyton relaxes onto her back, letting one hand float to the juncture between her thighs. Holy fuck, she's rubbing her clit with her middle finger. A groan pours out of me.

"That's so fucking sexy, baby." I moan, my eyes following the tiny circles her finger is making.

"Yeah?" She gives me a devious smile as if she doesn't know how unbelievably hot it is to watch her touch herself in my bed. Her eyes lock with mine, holding my gaze while she keeps up those lazy circles.

"Mmm. Yeah. But it's my turn now, angel."

I move her hand back to her side and replace it with mine, working her over with my thumb while my middle finger slides into her. It earns me a groan of approval. She's so goddamned wet, twitching and shaking underneath me. It's magnificent.

"So perfect," I say through a groan as I ease out of her, examining her glistening arousal on my fingers. My groin aches to have the same sheen. "Fuck," is all I can manage to say after seeing how wet she is. So I position myself above her, my erection pushing against the wet heat between her thighs. "Is this okay?"

"Go slow, okay?" she whispers. "It's been a while."

I nod, promising to take things at her speed. Slow and steady. I'll give her what she wants, a little at a time.

As gently as I can, I press the head of my cock against her opening, testing the waters, and she gasps and contracts against the bit of length I've given her. She's definitely tight, but keeping up the circles with my thumb allows her muscles to relax into me. I think I can give her a little more, if she feels ready.

"Talk to me, okay?" I try to hold back the need building in my groin. I don't want her to feel like we have to go any further if she doesn't want to. I'm aching to be all the way inside her, but it's not up to me. She's running this show, and I'll let her tell me what she needs. "More?"

"Mmm, yes, more," she says on a groan.

I'm happy to oblige. I tilt my hips forward, letting my length slide into her. *Holy fuck.* She feels every bit as good as I imagined, and more. I have to bite my lip just to hang on to my control.

After a few of my slow, introductory thrusts, she finds her pace, rocking her hips and letting me hit a deeper spot within her. God fucking damn, I can't get enough of her. She crosses her legs behind my back and I lean into her, kissing down her neck as I bury myself in her, pulling a needy moan from her lips.

"Fuck, baby. So good." I'm normally better with words than this, but she's leaving me near speechless. Her gorgeous, full breasts bounce as I pump into her a little faster, and I can't help but lean in and take one in my mouth, sucking and running my tongue along one nipple while pinching the other.

"Josh, yes," she whimpers, her long, thick eyelashes fluttering against her cheeks. She's entering that state of bliss I've grown so fond of watching her slip into.

But I want more. I want to see her come undone while I'm inside her. And by the way her breath escalates each time I slide into her, I think I'm going to get what I want.

My thumb finds her clit again, stroking it in time with each thrust. She twitches and contracts against my touch. Yup. I've got her where I want her, right on the edge.

"Go ahead, angel. You know what I want. Show me how you come for me."

And she does. Hard and wild.

Her hands cling to my sheets for dear life as she unravels, contracting around me. She feels like heaven. And I'm right behind her, pouring into her, her name falling off my lips as I do.

Entirely drained, I collapse onto her momentarily, holding her tight against me as we catch our breath.

"Wow," she pants. "That was incredible."

"*You* are incredible." I press a grateful kiss to her flushed cheek before carefully easing out of her. "I'll be right back, okay?"

It's a quick trip down the hall to the bathroom, where I ditch the condom and wash my hands as I try to cool down. When I get back to the bedroom, Peyton is curled up in the center of my bed, her dark hair splayed across the pillows.

"Hey there, sleepyhead." I tug on a fresh pair of boxers and pull a T-shirt from my dresser, offering it to my snuggly guest. "Here, gorgeous. Put this on. It can get kind of chilly at night."

Peyton sits up in bed and raises a brow at me.

"Am I spending the night?"

I can't help but laugh. "Well, it sure looks like you are to me. But I'm happy to drive you home if you'd prefer."

She eyes the T-shirt a moment longer, then accepts it from me and pulls it over her head. It's a little too big and looks adorable hanging off her shoulders. I'll have to remember to let her keep it.

She moves from the center of the bed, making room for me to join her. I lace my arms around her waist, tugging her into me until she's nestled against my frame, and bury my nose in her hair.

"Sweet dreams, Peyton," I whisper, pressing a kiss into the back of her head. But she doesn't respond. She's already fast asleep in my arms.

It feels like hardly a nanosecond passes before I'm rudely awakened by the irritating, generic ringtone of my phone. Blinking, I check the clock on my nightstand.

Shit, it's morning already? Eight thirty a.m., to be exact. I should have been in the office half an hour ago, at the latest.

I spring out of bed and lunge for my phone, picking it up on the last ring. "Hello, this is Josh."

"Damn straight, it better be Josh." It's Brody. But not just any Brody. An incredibly pissed-off Brody. "I don't know who the hell else would have this phone. But then again, who knows with you lately?"

I scrub my hand through my hair, trying to wrap my head around what he means by that blow. I decide not to acknowledge it.

"Sorry, I overslept. I was beat from the trip this weekend. But I'll be in as soon as I can, I promise."

By this point, Peyton is half awake, looking at me curiously through hooded eyes. She looks so fucking cute with her hair all messy from a good night's sleep.

I wish I could crawl back into bed with her and treat her to some morning sex. But I don't have time for that, as much as it pains me. I need to get to the office and get my shit together for her product launch.

"Whatever. See you soon." Brody doesn't even wait for a response before hanging up.

I sigh, throwing my phone onto the bed and

rubbing the sleep out of my eyes. There are a lot of ways I would have liked to wake up this morning. This sure as hell wasn't one of them.

"Who was that?" Peyton asks, blinking against the sun seeping in through the blinds.

"Brody, wondering where I am. I overslept, and we have a ton of work to do before we launch your boxes next week. I need to get a move on, or I think he might bite my head off the second I step through the office doors."

She turns toward the clock to confirm what I told her. It's 8:35 already. I need to book it if I'm going make it to the office before ten.

"I shouldn't have come," Peyton mutters, climbing out of bed to find her things.

Fuck, no. That's not what I meant.

"Don't say that," I say. "I'm so glad you came. Please don't make this out to be your fault. It's not the end of the world that I'm a little late to the office."

"That's not the point." Her voice catches in her throat. "The point is that I'm standing in the way of business getting done. We said we'd keep things professional, and then we didn't. And now I'm getting in the way of your work, and Brody's upset, and . . . and where are my clothes?"

"In the living room. I'll get them." I start for the door, but she stops me before I get there.

"I've got it. You need to get ready for work."

I sigh. She's right, but I don't want to admit that. Work is important, but so is making sure Peyton doesn't walk out of my door feeling like we made a mistake.

"Fine. But no leaving until I can call you a ride home, all right?"

She nods in agreement, then slips out the door to find her clothes. I call for an Uber, then speed shower the smell of sex off of me, brush my teeth, and throw on whatever work clothes I can find that aren't dirty from our trip. All in record time.

Fifteen minutes later, I'm ready to go. Peyton's waiting for me by the door, her jacket on and purse draped over her shoulder. She's wearing the same clothes as yesterday, having left the shirt I lent her folded up on the coffee table.

"Hang on to that for me." I nod toward the shirt as I pull on my jacket. "It looks good on you."

She scrunches her brow at me, so I pick up the

shirt myself and slip it into her purse. Lucky for me, she doesn't put up a fight about it. I imagine her wearing it to bed at night. A little bit of me she can slip on and remember our night together. I like the thought.

"Your ride is about here," I say, checking my phone for the driver's location. "I'm sorry I can't drive you myself. Are you going to be okay?"

Peyton looks down at her cuticles, picking at them nervously. "Let's just make sure we talk about this later, okay? About all of this?"

She gestures to the space between us, and I immediately close it, bringing my lips to her cheek for several soft, short kisses.

"Of course. We'll talk things through later. Just don't waste your time feeling guilty, all right?" I press my thumb into the dimple in her chin, tilting her head until her gaze meets mine. "Because you? Last night? That was all worth it to me."

Her smile is slight, but it's still a smile. And I'll take what I can get.

CHAPTER TWENTY

Josh

The second I step into the office, I can tell something is up. It's way quieter than it should be first thing in the morning, and there's a weird uneasiness hanging in the air that hits me straight in the gut. This isn't the friendly office environment that I've worked hard to build over the past couple of years. Everyone seems way on edge. Even Irene, the always-cheery receptionist, looks like she's just seen a ghost.

"Irene, what's going on?" I hang up my coat, double-checking that there's not a monster in the closet terrorizing my usually upbeat staff.

She gives me the slightest smile. "Oh, nothing," she says, but her eyes, which are wide and worried behind her red-framed glasses, tell a much different story. When I frown at her, she gives me the truth in a whisper. "I think you should go check on Brody. He's been on a tirade this morning."

Ah, fuck. A grumpy Brody is the last thing we need today. We're *this* close from having things up and running for Peyton's big launch next week, but we need every second of work time to make it happen.

I give Irene a grateful nod for the tip, then head toward my partner's office. He's hunched over his desk, his hands tapping at jet speed across his keyboard and his eyes glued to the screen.

I rap on the open door with my knuckles just to get his attention. "Hey, dude, everything all right?"

He greets me with a stare so pointed, it could knock me right over. "No, not everything is all right. You're an hour and thirty fucking minutes late."

"Whoa. I'm planning on staying late today, okay?" I hold up my hands in front of me in defense. "No need to sweat it. I've got it under control. We're gonna get everything done for this Wish Upon a Gift launch."

A gruff sound of discontent rumbles in the back of Brody's throat. "We're not doing the Wish Upon a Gift launch, Josh. It's off."

My stomach ties itself into a knot that would leave even a top-tier Boy Scout impressed. "What the fuck do you mean, it's off?"

Stepping deeper into the office, I slowly close the door behind me. Brody's mood has already left the office in a weird state. I don't want to make it worse by letting anyone overhear this shit. Especially since I'm having a hard time keeping my own volume down.

"It's off," Brody says. "Done. Kaput. I'm drafting the memo about it now. This product isn't right for our company. Our trip upstate made that abundantly clear."

I take a deep, cleansing breath, urging Brody to do the same, then settle into the chair opposite from him. "This is coming out of left field. I know you're in charge of new business, but our trip upstate went just fine. The store managers were all over the idea of a new product. We're going to take Peyton's company to the next level with this product launch."

"Sure we will." Brody scoffs. "If our point of

contact with the potential client can stop thinking with his dick."

My stomach is now at least triple-knotted. "The fuck did you just say?"

"You think we didn't notice?" Brody's voice cuts through the air with a sternness I've never heard from him. "The way she just had to ride with you everywhere on our trip upstate? And you were practically eye-fucking her in every meeting we had. I'm surprised none of the store managers said anything about it."

"Probably because they were too focused on her actual pitch." I do my best to keep my cool, but I'm biting the inside of my cheek to keep from snapping at him. I can't believe he would pull shit like this so late in the deal. "It's a good product, Brody. You should know, you're the one who found her company and wanted to work with her in the first place. And we both know we're fucked if we drop this deal now. We need something new to market around the holidays if we're going to stay competitive."

"Is that really what you're worried about?" he asks on a growl. "Because it seems like you're only concerned with keeping her close so you can move in on her."

Anger threatens to burst out of my throat, but I swallow it. What the hell is Brody's problem? We've been best friends since the first week of college, and we've never fought. Not over work, not over women, nada. We've been a united front since day one. Of all the times he's had the chance to get pissy with me, does it really have to be now?

"I believe in this product. The fact that Peyton is the one behind it has nothing to do with it."

"Bullshit. Prove it, then."

What does he want me to do? Dance around like a monkey? Dip my balls in hot sauce?

Fuck that. Everything I can think of sounds like it should be happening in a frat house, not our company's corporate headquarters. There's only one thing I can think of that will get my point across, and it's the last thing I want to offer. Unfortunately, I think it's all I've got.

"Fine. Take me off the project."

The words hang heavy in the air between us. Brody lifts a brow, looking for an explanation.

"Put me on the back end," I say. "You can be the point of contact with Peyton, and I'll do the dirty work on the internal side. Budgeting, negotiations with suppliers, all the shit you hate. I won't even talk to Peyton until the product launch is a massive success."

The second I realize what just came out of my mouth, I want to immediately take it all back. The idea of totally ghosting on Peyton for the next week is unfair to both of us. But then again, so is the idea of her losing out on this deal.

For better or worse, Brody is clearly interested in my proposition. He leans back in his chair and folds his arms over his chest as he considers my offer. "And what if it's not a massive success? What if it flops and it puts us in the red?"

I gulp down the lump in my throat. "It won't," I say matter-of-factly, but that's not enough of a defense to get Brody off my back.

"Thanks for the security blanket, Hanson, but your opinion doesn't sell products." Brody scowls as he swivels his chair back toward his desk, signaling the end of his interest in the conversation.

Bullshit. He's not just going to turn his back on me like that. Not as my business partner, and certainly not as my best friend.

If we don't close on this deal, I'll totally lose Peyton's trust, and Wine O'Clock will lose its competitive edge for the holiday season. And if Peyton turns around and takes her product to a different company, we'll lose out to them in terms of profit margins.

I can just imagine her working with one of our competitors, flirting over business meetings and sneaking off together at company events. It makes a vein in my forehead threaten to burst. On every front, I'm relying on this deal. I'm relying on Brody. I've got to use whatever last-ditch effort I can.

"How about I make you a deal?" I say.

Brody looks over his shoulder hesitantly, then swivels his chair back toward me, his hands folded neatly in his lap like he's some kind of mafia boss.

With one last deep breath, I make my pitch. "I do the dirty work. You be the point of contact. And if the launch is a bust, then I'll delete Peyton's number for good."

The offer sends Brody's eyebrows shooting up to his hairline with surprise. "Holy shit, dude. I said that you were thinking with your dick. I didn't say you had to swear off this girl altogether."

"I know," I say curtly. "And I won't have to. That's how confident I am that this product won't fail."

That's it. All my cards are on the table. I've offered up the best that I've got, even though the very thought of it makes me sick to my stomach. Giving up Peyton would be the biggest mistake of my life, but it's a mistake I won't have to make. There's not a doubt in my mind that her launch will be a huge success.

"So? Do we have a deal?"

I extend a hand toward Brody and he eyes it momentarily, then clasps it with his own. One firm handshake, and I've made yet another dangerous deal. One I know I could never keep, and I sure as hell hope that I won't have to.

CHAPTER TWENTY-ONE

Peyton

In the few short weeks that Josh and I have known each other, I didn't realize how much he's become a part of my daily routine. Whether we're meeting to discuss the details of our professional collaboration, or flirting via text after business hours, we've been constantly connected since the day I received that misdirected sext from him. Come to think of it, there hasn't been a single day since we met that he and I haven't checked in with each other.

At least, not until now.

Since my rushed exit from his apartment yesterday morning, I haven't heard a word from Josh. He hasn't replied to my texts, or even acknowledged the work-related emails I've copied him on. It's crazy how less than a month ago, I didn't even know this man existed. Now I go a day and a half without hearing from him, and I start to worry that he's fallen off the edge of the earth.

Maybe the silence wouldn't hurt quite so much had Josh and I not slept together for the first time less than forty-eight hours ago. I've had guys ghost on me after we've hooked up, but Josh doesn't seem like the type. And even if he is that kind of guy, we're going to be spending the next week together in the office pulling all-nighters to prepare for this launch. It's kind of hard to avoid someone when they're a foot away from you at a conference table.

As the elevator dings and opens on the Wine O'Clock offices, I step out onto the merlot-colored carpet and head straight for Josh's office. Brody probably put him on expense-report duty after he rolled in late yesterday. A giggle slips from my lips as I imagine him drowning under a gigantic pile of receipts and spreadsheets. That would certainly explain why he's been MIA.

I knock twice on Josh's office door, turning the handle when I get no immediate response. Instead of being greeted by Josh's knockout smile like usual, there's nothing to see here but the blue glow of a computer screen.

He's not here.

I pull up my phone calendar, verifying that we do, in fact, have a meeting today. Yup. *Two p.m., finalization of online marketing campaigns.*

It should be a quick one, considering all the hours Josh and I have already put in with the marketing team. I would be out of here in an hour, if Josh were actually on time. What's his deal with running late lately?

There's no point in sitting here in his empty office, so I head toward the conference room to settle in for our meeting. Most of the marketing team is already there, setting up a presentation of the finalized ads. At the head of the table, where Josh would normally sit, Brody is furiously shuffling through a stack of print ads, entirely oblivious to my entrance.

"Good morning," I say, and Brody looks up.

"Oh, good, right on time." He stands to hand me a stack of materials to review, then returns to his seat and his stack of paperwork. "We'll get started in just a minute."

Just a minute? Doesn't he realize we're still missing a crucial part of the team? If he's not going to broach the subject, I will.

"Where's Josh?" I scan the room, expecting him to come walking in any second now, coffee in hand, a bright smile on his gorgeous face. And after yesterday's fiasco, he'd better not be late again.

Brody loosens the knot of his tie as he opens his laptop, dodging my eye contact. "Josh is no longer the point of contact for you for this project."

I flinch in surprise. "What does that mean?"

"It means you'll be working with me instead of Josh from here up through the launch." Brody's tone is so matter-of-fact, like he's chatting about his commute instead of throwing a major curveball my way.

No more working with Josh? I'm equal parts confused and heartbroken. The thought of not working with Josh, not getting to watch the way his eyes dance when he comes up with a good idea or intentionally presses my knee against his during a meeting, leaves a hollow feeling in my chest.

"When was that change made?"

I know I'm at risk of sounding a little too interested in the subject, but I think I deserve to know, even just from a professional standpoint. Up until now, Josh has been my go-to guy for everything. He's handled all my contracts and negotiations, right down to reaching out to me for input on the packaging design. Brody has been more of a big-picture, behind-the-scenes type of guy. A change this major with only a week left until launch seems unnecessary, at the least, and risky at most.

"We made the swap yesterday morning," Brody says.

The words ring in my ears. Yesterday morning. As in right after I left Josh's place. There's no way that's just a coincidence.

"Any particular reason?"

The knot in my stomach is getting bigger and bigger by the second. I couldn't live with myself if I found out that Josh got cut from working with me because I made him late.

Brody smiles through his obvious annoyance with me. "Josh came in and asked to be taken off the launch, so I went ahead and made the change. Is that going to be a problem?"

"Of course not," I sputter, maybe a bit too quickly. "I was just curious. It's a big switch this close to the launch. But I understand."

What a big fat lie. I understand nothing. This makes as much sense to me as quantum physics. Why the hell would Josh specifically ask not to work with me? And more importantly, why didn't he mention this to me himself?

I'm tempted to give Brody the third degree and get to the bottom of this, but one more question out of me might tip him off that something's going on. Instead, I zip my lips and take a seat at the conference table, filing this away as a problem to deal with later. We've got a lot of ground to cover in this meeting. And my broken heart and bruised ego over a man ghosting on me after sex isn't something I can deal with at this precise moment.

Reviewing the digital marketing campaigns takes about three times as long as expected. Turns out, Brody was totally out of the loop on all the ground that Josh and I had already covered, which means an insane amount of backtracking and re-explaining our choices. It's infuriating, to say the least. All the momentum we gained on our trip upstate is suddenly gone, and without Josh steering things, it feels like we've taken three steps back. And with only seven days until boxes hit shelves. Lord help us.

Brody wraps things up just as the sun slips behind the Manhattan skyline, leaving the conference room bathed in an eerie orange twilight. How appropriate. Both Manhattan and I have been left totally in the dark this evening.

I'm not three steps out of the conference room when I whip out my phone and text Josh, asking for an explanation.

Peyton: Brody said you asked to be taken off the launch. Is there a reason you don't want to work with me anymore?

I can instantly see that he's read it, but I don't get so much as the three little dots suggesting he's going to grace me with a response. So, I try again.

Peyton: Seriously? You have nothing to say? Please, just tell me what's going on. Are we okay?

Again, he reads it, but no response. My stomach starts churning at top speed. Something is up, and I need to know what.

Pivoting on my heel, I head back to the conference room where Brody is chatting with the marketing director, still trying to make sense of an ad Josh and I came up with together.

"Hey, Brody?" I say, interrupting. "Do you know if Josh's phone is working?"

Brody's shoulders tense, his mouth forming a perfectly straight line. "Yeah. His phone is working fine. He just texted me a second ago."

My jaw clenches as I try to force a smile. Whatever is going on here, Brody is clearly in on it. And I don't like it one fucking bit.

"Could you let him know that I would like to speak with him, please?" I say tersely.

Brody's shoulders fall back into place as a long sigh leaks from his mouth. "Yeah," he mutters. "I'll tell him, Peyton."

I can tell by his voice that he means it. I can also tell that it's not going to make a difference. Josh fucking Hanson got what he wanted from me, and now he's disappearing.

Just like every other knuckle-dragging douchebag that came before him.

CHAPTER TWENTY-TWO

Peyton

Two weeks later

When my gift boxes hit store shelves last week, I had to remind myself over and over that good things take time. It took years of hard work to build my business to this point. Although this business deal was a huge step, it was just one step, not an escalator. At least, that's what I told myself.

And then, after a week of my products being stocked, the numbers came in. The glowing blogger reviews. The immediate demands for increased stock at nearly every store. A mere seven days later, and my cut of profits has already surpassed a whole year's worth of income from my online store.

Maybe good things take time, but it turns out, great things can happen in the blink of an eye.

"Another bottle of bubbly!" Libby calls out to the bartender on a laugh, and Sabrina encourages her by slamming what's left in her glass.

Needless to say, drinks are on me tonight.

I didn't even know Speakeasy had champagne available, but they've somehow dusted off whatever stock they have for us. With an echoing pop, the second bottle of the evening is opened, foaming out of the beer glasses we're drinking from, which was the closest thing to champagne flutes the bar could offer us. Champagne in a beer glass. I think it sums up the three of us perfectly.

"Say *cheese*!" I pass my phone off to one of the bartenders, and Libby tugs Sabrina and me into a tight hug, the three of us posing in front of the **CONGRATULATIONS, PEYTON!** banner they hung over our usual table.

"No, don't say cheese!" Sabrina says. "Say Wish Upon a Gift!"

The bartender snaps the picture, but when he passes my phone back to me, the result is anything but flattering. Turns out saying my company name doesn't make for quite the same smiles as saying *cheese* does. We all look like we're in the middle of chewing something tough.

"Oh my God, we need to retake it," Sabrina says, but I just laugh, instantly uploading the picture to Instagram and tagging them both.

"It's perfect," I tell them. "The perfect picture of a perfect night."

Well, almost perfect. Even amidst all the celebration, there's still a hollowness in my gut that no amount of champagne seems to fill. It's ridiculous that I'd feel anything but over the moon. I'm with my best friends at my favorite bar, celebrating the spectacular success of my company. What more could I possibly want?

My stomach shifts, and not from the champagne. I know exactly what more I want, but I can hardly admit it to myself.

It's Josh. I want Josh.

The realization instantly sobers me up. It's been two weeks now since I scrambled out of his bed, swearing that, although he may have doubled my personal orgasm record, sleeping with him was a mistake that could ruin everything.

That same day I was given a new point of contact at Wine O'Clock, and since then, he hasn't so much as texted me to check in. I thought that maybe he'd left the project so that things could be strictly personal, not professional, between the two of us. But instead? Nothing. Not a word.

The silence stings. Hell, I should hate him for it.

But somehow, deep in the bottom of my heart, I'm desperately hanging on to a *maybe*. Maybe it doesn't have to be this way. Maybe he's thinking of me too. Wanting me. Wondering if we had something worthwhile. Maybe, by some miracle, he's holding on to that *maybe* too.

"Peyton? Are you okay?"

I didn't realize I've been staring into my glass of champagne like it was a crystal ball that would tell me how I'm going to solve all of this. "What? Oh, no, it's nothing. I'm fine."

I force a tight smile, but Libby and Sabrina both give me identical knowing looks, completely not buying it.

"You're thinking about him again, aren't you?" Libby's smug smile tells me it's a question she already knows the answer to.

Normally, that joke would get at least a pity laugh out of me, but not right now. Instead, I just swirl the champagne in my glass, watching the bubbles pop and disappear. "I don't know. I'm just . . . sad? Pissed? Is there a word for that?"

"Sissed?" Libby suggests.

This gets a laugh out of all three of us. Then out of the blue, Sabrina's giggles come to an abrupt stop and the color quickly drains from her cheeks.

"You okay, Sabrina?"

She doesn't respond to me. Instead, she tugs on Libby's sleeve and whispers something in her ear, and suddenly, both of them look like a ghost just walked into the bar.

"Hey, Peyton? Can you pull up that picture of Josh? The one you showed us on the company website after your first meeting?"

Skeptical, I lift one eyebrow. "Um, sure? Why?"

I don't know what's gotten into them, but they're insistent on me pulling up his head shot, so I type in the website and hand them the phone. They huddle together to examine the picture, then look back up over my shoulder, then down at the screen again.

"Um, guys?" I try again. "Everything okay?"

"Depends," Libby whispers, drawing out the word cautiously. "Were you expecting Josh to show up here tonight?"

My stomach drops to my knees. "What the hell are you talking about?"

"She's talking about the fact that Mr. Left You on Read for Two Weeks is standing at the bar," Sabrina says. "Does he know that this is our spot?"

My head starts to spin with memories of telling Josh about girls' nights at Speakeasy. Did he actually remember, or is he just here by accident? Either way, they've got to be having a joint hallucination. There's no way in hell this is happening to me right now.

"Are you sure it's not just a doppelganger?" I ask, my voice dripping with desperation.

Libby shakes her head. "I would recognize that jawline anywhere."

"And damn, he's hot as fuck." Sabrina's lips pinch together. "Sorry. I realize that was poorly timed."

I suck in a deep breath, chasing it with the rest of my champagne. "All right. I'm gonna look."

With as much subtlety as I can manage, I glance over my shoulder and immediately lock eyes with him. He's wearing the same suit jacket he had on when we pitched to the stores upstate. Underneath it is a bright blue shirt that makes his eyes absolutely sparkle.

Screw him for looking so damn handsome.

He's leaning against the bar, martini glass in hand, but whatever he's drinking doesn't hold his attention. By the way he's staring me down, his focus isn't on drinking tonight.

"Yup, that's him." My heart is threatening to leap into my throat. "What do I do?"

"Go talk to him," Sabrina and Libby say in unison.

Like it's that easy. I want to bury my face in my hands, but I don't want that asshole to see how much he's messed with my head. He doesn't deserve that kind of power trip. Not tonight when I'm supposed to be celebrating.

"What am I even supposed to say? 'Fuck you very much for completely ghosting on me'?"

Panic flickers in Libby's eyes. "Whatever you want to say, you'd better think fast. He's walking this way."

Next thing I know, I can feel a presence towering behind me, the familiar smell of a summer storm, although fall is nearly over. It's him. I guess there's no escaping now.

"Good evening, ladies," Josh says, his voice low and as sweet as the breeze. I hate that it sends goose bumps climbing up my arms. "You must be Sabrina and Libby. I've heard so much about you. I'm Josh, one of Peyton's business partners."

Is that all we are? Because it felt like a fuck of a lot more when he was inside me. I hold my breath, trying to suffocate the butterflies in my stomach.

"We know who you are," Libby murmurs through pursed lips, earning her a swat on the arm from Sabrina.

"Do you mind if I steal Peyton for a moment? I don't mean to interrupt your evening, because I'm sure you must be celebrating Peyton's success."

"Steal me?" I blurt out, jumping to my feet and whirling to face him. "Why are you even here? You're the one who's been avoiding me like the freaking plague."

I'm not usually one to lash out like this. Maybe it's the champagne or the heartbreak, or a mixture of both. But, *seriously*, unless he's here to beg for forgiveness, I have nothing to say to him right now. Actually, I have a lot to say to him, but none of it is very ladylike.

By the way Josh wrinkles his forehead, he clearly didn't mean it as a joke. "Things have just been complicated."

"That is such a line," I snap. "You're exactly like every other douchebag I've dated before. You only wanted me to think you were sweet and sensitive so you could sleep with me and then bail."

"Peyton, please. Listen to me." He's speaking under his breath, trying to avoid drawing any more attention from the bar than we already have. "Listen, I don't know what Brody told you, but I think there's been a misunderstanding."

I fist my hands, praying he can't hear the quiver in my voice as well as I can. "Brody made it quite clear you wanted nothing to do with me. And if that's what it means to *keep it professional*, then you're not nearly as business savvy as you pretend to be."

My throat is constricting, and it's all I can do to

hold back the tears. I won't do this. I won't let him see me cry.

Composing myself, I continue. "And yeah. There's been a misunderstanding," I manage to say through my sniffles. "Because you seem to think you can disappear from my life and come back when it's convenient for you, when I'm a bottle of champagne in and you think you can get me to sleep with you again. *That*, Josh, is a massive misunderstanding."

The second I feel a tear spill down my cheek, I grab my purse and storm out the door, booking it toward the nearest subway station before the waterworks start. I feel bad for leaving without paying our tab, but there's no looking back now. Sabrina and Libby will understand.

I have to get away from here, away from him.

CHAPTER TWENTY-THREE

Peyton

"Can we come in?" a familiar voice calls from the other side of my bedroom door.

After my emergency evacuation from Speakeasy, I should have known that Libby and Sabrina would follow me home. What I don't know is if I'm ready to have company yet.

Instead of replying to their knocks, I scoop up another bite of double-chocolate-fudge ice cream and pop the spoon into my mouth, doing my best not to drip any on the comforter. I don't need a stain on my sheets reminding me of Josh's affinity for ice cream. As it is, I can't even enjoy this ice cream without thinking about how it's his favorite food.

Screw him for making me think of him when I'm trying to mope. Can't a girl eat her feelings without being reminded of the man she's trying to get over?

"Peyton. You're gonna have to pee eventually," Sabrina calls from outside the door. "Either you can let us in now, or we'll stand here and wait until you have to open this door."

I groan, dropping my spoon into my half-empty pint. She's right, but I'm not happy about it. Setting the ice cream on my nightstand, I pull myself out of bed and unlock the door to let them in.

"Oh, honey, are you okay?" Sabrina's face scrunches up as she takes in the sight of me in all my breakup glory. The mascara trailing down my cheeks, the messy bun on top of my head, and wearing my coziest pajamas.

The second I got home from the bar, I grabbed the pint of ice cream I've stored in the freezer for a rainy day and took the stairs two at a time, yelling out to Gram that *no, I don't want to talk about it*. Gram has been crazy obsessed with the idea of Josh and me together. How am I supposed to tell her that he's just another asshole who wanted to get in my pants?

"Girl, you don't really want to be alone right now, do you?" Libby asks, flopping down across my bed. "You don't need to do that to yourself."

"She's right." Sabrina shakes the plastic grocery bag in her hand. "What you need is more ice cream. Which we have graciously provided."

"And makeup wipes!" Libby pulls a package of them from the plastic bag and tosses them my way. Sabrina gives her a weird look, but Libby just shrugs. "What? I figured she might need one. Sue me for being prepared."

I drag a makeup wipe across my cheeks, the clean coolness of it feeling like a fresh start. Which is something I could really use right now.

Once I'm cleaned up, I toss the wipe and settle back onto the bed with my girls. As much as I wanted to wallow in sadness by myself, I'm happy I gave in and let them in. Having them here makes me feel less empty.

"Thanks for coming, guys," I say, exhaling slowly.

"Here, finish this and tell us what's on your mind." Sabrina hands me what's left of my pint of ice cream, then leans back against the pillows, ready to hear whatever I have to say.

The only problem is that I don't know where to start. My head is in a million places at once, and I don't know how to make sense of any of it.

"I just . . . I thought he was different, you know? And then when we finally sleep together, he totally ghosts on me? And then *shows up* without *notice*? I mean, who does that?"

"Men," Libby and Sabrina say in unison, which makes them giggle.

Meanwhile, I'm near the end of this pint and hoping there's an explanation at the bottom. If not, I'll be forced to move on to the next pint.

"Maybe he has a good explanation, who knows?" Libby says as she takes the lid off another pint of double-chocolate fudge and passes it my way.

"Yeah, or maybe he's just exactly like every other guy I've ever dated." As I plunge my spoon into the softened chocolatey goodness, I can't help but remember that these aren't the kind of pints I thought I'd be throwing back tonight. We should be celebrating my business success, not moping in my bedroom. Fuck Josh for taking this night away from me.

"You won't know unless you talk to him," Libby says. "If he's ballsy enough to walk up to you at a bar, I think he'll probably have the guts to actually answer your calls this time."

"Well, yeah." I shrug, licking chocolate off my lower lip. "He's already called me three times tonight. So I'm guessing he's probably willing to talk things out."

Their jaws practically hit the comforter at that update.

"He's been calling you?" Sabrina's screech is so high-pitched, I'm surprised our neighbors' dogs don't start barking. "Why didn't you say that earlier? Did you pick up or what?"

"No, of course not." Frowning, I take another bite. "What would I even say to him right now? The only men I want to talk to are Ben and Jerry."

Both my friends roll their eyes. I guess I deserve that.

"You don't want to talk to him, but you're mad that he wouldn't talk to you? That doesn't add up," Sabrina says, giving me a pointed look.

Defensively, I take an enormous bite of ice cream so I don't have to respond to that.

"She's still mourning, Sabrina. Cut her some

slack." Libby throws a pillow at Sabrina, who swiftly ducks it. "Here's what I think. I think he's either calling to apologize to you or to explain himself. But it's up to you to decide if you want to hear it or not. Because it could be legit, or it could be total bullshit."

"Right now, this all feels like bullshit." I whine, passing my ice cream to Libby so I can bury my face in a pillow.

Maybe if I hide from this whole mess it'll just go away. When I take my head out of this pillow, maybe we'll be back at Speakeasy, just me and my girls, celebrating the success of my company without the added trouble of trying to piece my broken heart back together.

I peer out cautiously. Nope. No luck. Still in my bedroom, still brokenhearted. Damn. It was worth a shot.

"Okay, look," Sabrina says bluntly, folding her arms over her chest. "You're allowed to be mopey for the rest of the night. Eat your ice cream and pout, and watch all the sad romantic movies you want. But come tomorrow, you have to give this some actual thought and decide if you want to give this guy a chance or not." Before I have a chance to respond, she adds, "And if you decide not to give him a shot, you have to promise to move on. Like, for real. Which includes dating someone new. Deal?"

I suck in a deep breath. The idea of moving on and dating another man sounds like the worst kind of torture, but I know she's right. "Deal."

I wake up to the smell of chocolate-chip pancakes wafting in through my door.

Sabrina and Libby stayed pretty late last night, but they must have given Gram the rundown on what happened before they left, because there's no other reason Gram would be cooking my all-time favorite comfort food.

I can barely hear the sound of some pop song I've never heard before playing on the kitchen speaker. Gram is shamelessly singing along, but she's not the only one. A low, gravelly voice joins in. It's Duncan, I realize. I guess she needed a cooking buddy.

A quick glance in my mirror tells me that a good night's sleep did me some good. The puffiness around my eyes has subsided, and thanks to Libby coming to the rescue with her makeup wipes, my mascara trails are long gone. I might even pass as someone who's doing okay.

Despite all that, there's no fooling Gram. If I so much as step into the kitchen, I'm going to have to talk about it. But I can't resist chocolate-chip pancakes.

"Good morning, sleepyhead." Gram is steadying herself on her walker with one hand while flipping a pancake on the griddle with the other. She's recovered enough that she doesn't need the walker much anymore, but I appreciate her being smart. "Duncan, darling, could you pour this girl a cup of coffee? I think she needs it."

Duncan stands up from his seat at the table, following Gram's request. I watch as his shaky hand grabs a mug, pouring it to the brim. He's wearing some gray plaid pajama pants that perfectly match his silver hair. When I look back at Gram, I see she has on a similar pair.

Matching PJs. These two couldn't get cuter if they tried.

"Here you go, sweetie," Duncan says, passing me a hot mug of coffee. "I'll let you fix it up the way you like."

As I add my cream and sugar, he piles up a stack of chocolate-chip pancakes for me and sets it at the empty setting at the table.

"You guys are spoiling me," I mutter under my breath after taking my first sip of coffee and sitting down in front of my pancakes. They smell like heaven.

"Sabrina and Libby told me you might need a little spoiling," Gram says, turning down the volume on her pop music.

I can hardly suppress my eye roll. I knew those girls wouldn't keep their mouths shut. Not that I wouldn't have filled Gram in myself eventually.

She scoots her walker over to the table and snags the seat between Duncan and me as I busy myself with cutting my pancakes with the side of my fork, hoping to avoid this conversation as long as possible.

"Pass the syrup, please?"

Gram reaches across the table to grab the sticky brown bottle, then holds it up in the air above her head. "No syrup unless you agree to talk about it."

I scowl at her, but she doesn't budge. The woman knows me too freaking well. "Fine, I'll talk." I reach out and she passes the bottle over, then folds her hands on the table expectantly, ready to listen.

Between bites of pancake, I give Gram and Duncan the abbreviated version of the tragic tale of Josh and Peyton, skipping over the part where he and I slept together the night before he made his grand exit from my life. I'll let them assume what they want, but no way am I saying that, especially not in front of Duncan. I also leave out the fact that we technically *met* before ever being introduced at the office. No reason to let them know about the dick pic either, I decide.

"In summary," I say with a sigh, "the guy disappeared just as I was starting to fall for him. And now he's suddenly showing up again, and I don't know what I'm supposed to think."

Gram raises a brow at me. "So you admit that you were falling for him, huh?"

My shoulders drop as I stare down at my syrupy plate. "Yeah. I really was."

She cocks her head. "Was? Or still are?"

The question weighs on my heart heavier than I'd like to admit. "I don't know."

Gram chuckles, shaking her head. "It sounds

like there's a lot of things you don't know. I think it might help if you talked to him, sweetie. Maybe you'd find out a thing or two."

Duncan nods in agreement, then reaches over the table and grabs Gram's hand, giving it a squeeze. "Trust me. Talking things out is always the best way. When your Gram told me she spent that whole work thingamajig at the hotel dancing with that other fella, I was so jealous, I swear I turned green. But that's because she didn't have a chance to tell me why."

Gram's eyes crinkle as a soft smile spreads across her face. "Because if I didn't stop hanging around Josh and Peyton, they never would've had any alone time that night. Plus, they were playing mine and Duncan's song. I couldn't miss that."

"The point is," Duncan says, "if you really care about a person, you need to let them tell their whole story. Because if you don't, you may be losing them somewhere in the details."

"And if you love somebody," Gram adds, "there's nothing in this world worth losing them for."

CHAPTER TWENTY-FOUR

Josh

It's been a full week since I strolled into Speakeasy, expecting to join in on a legendary celebration. The Wish Upon a Gift launch was a total success, meaning I was finally free from that stupid deal I made with Brody.

My plan for the evening was foolproof: surprise Peyton at her favorite bar, meet her best friends, and then take her home with me for some much-deserved celebrating one-on-one. Instead, I was greeted with the tongue-lashing of a lifetime. So, yeah, just about the opposite of what I had in mind.

Even with a week to recover, my ego is still a little bruised from being rejected so completely by a woman I miss on the daily. Unfortunately, that's the least of my worries. I'm torn the fuck apart over the thought that I obviously hurt her. But I had no choice, and I need to make her understand that.

I thought I was doing the right thing by backing away from the project. Brody would have evidence of how much I believed in Peyton's product, Peyton would have the professional work environment that I couldn't give her, and once the launch was over with, I thought we would pick things up where we left off. Boom. Perfect. Everyone wins.

I knew it wouldn't be easy—hell, I missed her like crazy during those two weeks of silence. Not to mention my dick had to be reintroduced to my hand in a big, bad way. But it was worth it to see Peyton and her business succeed, and I was so sure she'd understand.

And maybe she will, if she ever answers my calls and gives me a chance to explain.

After putting in a few good hours of tossing and turning, I give the finger to the sheep I've been counting. I'm wide awake. I swear to God, I've been running on nothing but energy drinks and a fucking prayer since things with Peyton fell apart. And it's starting to look like I won't know what a REM cycle feels like again until I sort my shit out.

It's un-fucking-pleasant, to say the least.

Unplugging my phone from its place charging on my bedside table, I opt to endure tonight's episode of insomnia by scrolling through my contacts, looking for anyone I can go to for advice. Brody sure as hell isn't the one to ask about this situation. Even if he weren't so involved, I need womanly advice, not bro advice.

When I get to the Cs in my contact list, one name sticks out to me. It's so obvious. There's only one person who saw Peyton and me together as a couple, not as business partners. My cousin Claire.

My thumb hovers over her name as I weigh my options. Claire is all the way upstate. Not exactly a quick trip to discuss my woman problems. But there's no harm in shooting her a text to see if she's free. Maybe she'll get back to me in the morning.

My phone buzzes immediately. Looks like I won't have to wait that long.

Claire is up with the baby, and although she agrees that I'm insane for wanting to drive all the way up there, she promises to be home and ready to listen if I have an emergency to talk out. That's all I need to hear to hop in my car and head north.

Yeah, driving six hours for relationship advice

seems a little insane. But then again, so does continuing to lose sleep over Peyton. And if anyone can help me make sense of this mess, it's Claire.

Six and a half hours of hugging the left lane later, I'm back where I was a few weeks ago—standing on Claire's doorstep, the doorbell chiming its usual tune. It makes me wish Peyton were standing here with me again.

To my surprise, there's no herd of excited kiddos sprinting up to the door this time, though. Just Claire, gripping a mug of coffee and shaking her head, the slightest smile on her lips.

"You really did it. You drove all the way up here." She sounds equal parts shocked and delighted. "Come on in. Whatever you need to talk about that was worth that drive, I think I need to be sitting down to hear it."

Inside the house, it doesn't take long for me to see why I didn't get my usual stampede greeting at the door. Claire's husband is home for the day, and he and the kids are lounging in front of the TV, watching some movie with talking animated cars. He gives me a wave from where he's planted on the floor with little Connor in his lap, who is running a toy car along his dad's thigh.

"I put him on kid duty," Claire whispers as she hands me a full coffee mug.

Thank God. I'm exhausted from that drive.

With the living room occupied, and the kitchen close enough that the little ones would be within earshot, I suggest we take advantage of the nice weather and move this conversation outside. Claire agrees, and I follow her out through the sliding glass door and onto the patio. Although the last thing I want to do is sit after being in a car for so long, I politely take a seat in the Adirondack chair across from her.

We're quiet for a moment, which gives me a chance to get a few sips of coffee in me before I launch into my mess of a story. As we sit here, I can't help but reminisce about the last time I was on this patio, introducing Peyton to the kids and watching them race to the playset. I'd be called a rotten egg all over again to have her here with me again.

My heart swells at the memory of how good she was with the kids, how she didn't even think twice about getting her nice dress dirty. She said she wants to come back here. Or at least wanted. The thought of that being in the past tense puts a knot in my stomach.

"So," Claire says, putting an end to my daydream. "What's going on, and why do I have a feeling it has to do with the girl you brought here?"

I snicker into my coffee. "Busted. But yeah, it's gotten complicated."

Claire stifles a giggle. "Complicated? Wasn't it already complicated that you and your business partner were so totally into each other?"

"Was it that obvious? We were trying to hide it."

This time, she doesn't even bother trying to hide her laugh. "Yeah, it was incredibly obvious. The way you two looked at each other? That's not how you look at a coworker. Anyone with eyes could see that."

"Yeah, and that was the problem." I sigh, working a hand through my hair. "I guess people caught on. Well, Brody did, at least. He got all riled up and was going to put an end to our deal with her company. So I kinda had to play hardball."

A crease forms across Claire's forehead. "Define hardball."

"Well, after Peyton, you know, spent the night for the first time, I overslept, and Brody pitched a fit. So she was worried that us being together would get in the way of work stuff. And then Brody comes at me with this *how are you gonna prove you're not thinking with your dick* bullshit. Long story short, I made him a deal where I'd back off the project and stop talking to Peyton until the launch was done."

Claire's eyes bulge, and her chin drops to her chest. "You slept with her and then you stopped talking to her? Are you kidding me?"

"It wasn't permanent. Just for two weeks, give or take. It was for the good of the business, she has to know that," I explain, my tone turning defensive. "And it was so Brody would believe me when I said this deal would be a success. This way, I could keep things professional, like she wanted. I was trying to help."

Claire blinks at me in disbelief, her mouth hanging open a solid two inches. "Um, question . . . When did you inform her of this brilliant plan?"

I recoil. "Sorry, what?"

Claire squeezes her eyes shut and inhales sharply. She's obviously trying to stop herself from yelling at me, but whether that's for my benefit or the kids', I'm not sure.

"Listen, Josh," she says in what's obviously

a forced calm tone. "A woman left your bed feeling insecure about your relationship. Your job is to soothe those worries, to make things right with her. Instead, your solution was to completely ignore her for two weeks?"

"Well, I guess when you put it like that . . ."

"What do you mean 'when you put it like that'? That's what you did. It doesn't matter that there was some kind of professional reasoning behind it. All you did was confirm that poor girl's worst fears—that she's a one-time fuck who means nothing to you."

"But she's not," I snap, as if Claire were the one I'm trying to convince.

Claire rests her mug on the arm of the chair and folds her arms across her chest. "And how is she supposed to know that?"

An insane amount of pressure starts building in my chest. *Fuck.* She's right.

There's no way in hell for Peyton to know that. Because all I did was disappear and then crash her celebration at Speakeasy without an explanation. And I never thought to ask Brody about how he broke the news of my disappearance to Peyton. For all I know, he might have said I was dead. Or worse, seeing someone else.

"You need to call her, Josh," Claire says, leaning forward in her chair and laying a reassuring hand on my shoulder.

"No shit." I snort, shrugging her hand off of me. "I already tried that. She won't even pick up. She doesn't want to hear a word I have to say."

Claire rolls her eyes and folds one leg over the other, then crosses her arms again. She looks like the world's most annoyed pretzel. "Listen. I can't tell you how to fix it. I wish I could, because I really liked Peyton." Her face softens, probably at the memory of the two of us goofing around with her kids on the playset. "But I will say this. If Peyton is half as wonderful as she seemed when I met her, she's not going to stay single for very long. Girls like that get snatched up quick."

My gut tightens like I just took a punch to the stomach. "What, are you saying you think she's already moved on?"

Claire shrugs. "I don't know. I'm just saying it's not out of the realm of possibility. So, whatever you do, you'd better do it fast."

I give up on sipping my coffee and slam what's left in the mug, then check my watch. "Is seven hours from now fast enough?"

Claire's eyebrows shoot up to her hairline. "Are you telling me you're gonna turn your ass back around and drive back to Manhattan already?"

When she says it out loud, it makes me sound like a lunatic. But judging by the feeling in my gut, it's what I need to do. I need to talk to Brody and find out what he said to Peyton when I left the front end of the project. I need to know what kind of damage I need to repair in order to win this girl back.

That is, if I'm not too late.

"First, you're going to take a nap," Claire tells me, rising to her feet. "And then I'll see if I can help you make a plan."

I nod and follow her inside.

CHAPTER TWENTY-FIVE

Josh

In our time running this business, Brody and I have logged more than our fair share of Saturday night meetings. As co-founders of the company, we don't get the luxury of keeping work to a Monday through Friday grind. The one perk? When you're the boss, there's nobody to stop you from swapping out an office chair for a bar stool.

When I call Brody on my drive home and suggest we grab a drink tonight, I can tell by his attitude that he's expecting an evening of more work than play.

And he's not far off the mark. We can't talk about what went down between Peyton and me without talking through the details of the last few weeks of work. But little does Brody know that we won't be chatting about profit margins or marketing plans tonight. We've got much bigger fish to fry.

I'm a few sips away from polishing off my first well-deserved beer of the night when Brody makes his entrance. A glass of whiskey neat is already waiting for him on the other side of the table. I can be a good friend sometimes.

"You look exhausted, dude," Brody says as he slides into his seat.

I scoff. "Not even a *hi, how are ya*? Some friend you are."

I tap my longneck bottle against his glass, then down the rest of my beer as he samples his whiskey. The hops go down smooth and easy, taking the edge off the twelve and a half hours I've spent behind a steering wheel today.

Brody and I spend a few minutes shooting the shit, catching up on the ins and outs of our everyday lives. It's been a while since we've talked as friends instead of business partners. He tells me he's been spending more time at the gym, even when I'm not there to make him lift heavy. I'm glad he's been doing just as well outside of the office as in it. I wish I could say the same for me.

"Enough about me," Brody says, wincing from another sip of whiskey. "What's going on with you, man? You look like you were hit by a bus. You need to get laid or something?"

I slouch into my seat, killing the last swig of my beer. "I wish it were that easy. Actually, I need to clear the air with you about what went down with Peyton. I need to know what exactly you told her."

Brody squints at me, trying to get a read on my intentions. "What? Are you seriously that hung up on her or something?"

"Just answer the question, Brody."

He looks up at the ceiling, drumming his fingers on the table as he tries to remember, then gives up with a sigh and a shrug. "Sorry, man. I really don't think I remember the exact conversation."

"Well, think a little harder," I growl, causing Brody to flinch at my sudden shift in mood.

"Sheesh." He snorts, then thinks on it another second. "I don't know, something along the lines of you asking me to take you off the project."

I pause, waiting for him to keep going. But no,

that's all he's got. *Great.*

"That was it? You just told her I didn't want to work with her anymore? Nothing else?"

My best friend is looking at me like I'm sprouting a second head. "Uh, yeah? I just told her the truth. You told me you weren't going to be the point of contact anymore. And when she asked about you not responding to her texts, I just told her she probably wouldn't be hearing from you in a while."

Jesus Christ. Brody might be savvy as hell in the business world, but sometimes, I think this dude must be socially inept. Thanks to him, I may as well say sayonara to my relationship.

If I can even call it a relationship. I'm starting to question whatever it was that Peyton and I had.

What do you call it when you start catching feelings for your business partner? A fling? A flirtation? No, it was more than that. But no matter how you label it, it's long gone now.

"Thanks a lot, numbnuts." I sigh, nodding at the bartender to bring me another beer. "Now she hates my fucking guts."

"Why do you care? I thought you didn't want to talk to her anymore."

"Are you fucking kidding me? Did you listen to a word I had to say that day I was late to the office?" When I snap at him, he gives me a look of utter confusion.

Can he seriously be this oblivious?

"I told you I was pulling myself back from the project to show you how much I believed in her product," I say, trying to wrestle my temper back under control. "That I was so sure her boxes would be a success that I was willing to bet my relationship with her on it."

Brody goes wide-eyed, like this is the first time he's heard any of this. "Shit, dude, my bad. I misunderstood. I guess I had some serious Swiss-cheese brain going on with all the craziness of the launch."

I have about a hundred insults ready to hurl his way about having no brain at all, but the bartender interrupts by delivering my beer. Just in the nick of time. I guess there's no point losing my cool with Brody anyway. He may be clueless, but it's not like he was trying to fuck things up for me.

I take a long swig, hoping the beer will drown my anger. "Well, I guess that's that," I mutter, wiping my mouth with the side of my hand. "One stupid miscommunication, and I've lost the woman I love."

Brody recoils at my word choice. "Whoa, man. You're really using the L-word on this girl?"

Shit, did I really just say that I love her? I hadn't even thought it through all the way. The words just kinda came out.

I suck in a long, slow inhale, trying to make sense of all the emotions racing through my skull. I haven't said that word out loud in a long time. And maybe it's a bit fast. But when you get that buzzing feeling deep in your chest, you can't just ignore it. And every time I think about Peyton, that's what I feel.

"Yeah. I think I am. No . . . I *know* I am. I love Peyton. And I've got to find a way to get her back."

Damn, it feels good to say that out loud.

A smile threatens the corner of Brody's mouth. "Damn. All right. Go get her, man. Do you have a plan or anything?"

I shake my head. "Nope. But I know that you owe me one. So you're gonna help me."

"Me? How the hell am I supposed to help?" Brody laughs. "My permanently single ass doesn't know a damn thing about winning over women."

Damn. He's right. As much as I'd like him to get me out of this bullshit he launched me into, I don't think he's the solution. I'm going to need the help of someone with more relationship know-how, someone who knows Peyton like the back of their hand.

And then it hits me. I'm going to need to get Gram on my side.

I snap my fingers. "I've got it. I know what I have to do."

Glancing at my watch, I realize I don't have much time if I want to do something about it tonight. It's already getting late. But if the past few weeks are any indication, I won't be sleeping tonight unless I take some action.

After slamming what's left of my beer, I jump to my feet. "I've got a phone call to make. Cool if I bounce?"

Brody waves me off toward the door. "Of course. I got the tab." He snickers, suppressing a smile. "Least I can do, right?"

I'm hardly out the door when I start scrolling through my missed calls, hoping for a miracle. I'm sure that Peyton has called me from Gram's phone once before when hers was dead.

Bingo. A number with the same area code as Peyton's. I cross my fingers and hit the CALL button.

"Hello?"

Yup. That's Gram.

I clear my throat, suddenly realizing I haven't thought through what I was going to say. "Um, hi, Gram. I mean, Mrs. . . . Gram. It's Josh."

The line is quiet for a second, and I'm worried I crossed a line by calling her. But then her usual spirited tone returns to the call, slightly quieter than before.

"You can call me Gram, sweetie. That's just fine. It's good to hear from you. What can I do for you?"

Slipping into my car for a little privacy, I give her the abridged version of my side of the story. She's probably gotten an earful from her granddaughter about what an asshole I am. And based on what Brody said to Peyton when I backed off the project, I deserve to be called every name in the book.

Gram doesn't have much reason to believe me when I tell her that this was all a misunderstanding, but I've got all my fingers and toes crossed that she'll hear me out on this. When I realize I've been rambling for a minute straight, I catch my breath and cut to the chase.

"Long story short, I just want to know if she's okay," I say, "and if I stand a chance at a second shot with her. Unless she's already, you know, found someone new."

Gram's quiet again. *Damn it.* She's probably trying to figure out how to break the news of Peyton's much hotter, much nicer boyfriend who has entered the picture.

Fuck. I drag a hand through my hair, trying to hold the phone far enough from me that Gram won't hear my heartbeat pounding in my chest.

And then she breaks the silence with two sentences that lift the weight of nearly a full month of sleepless nights from my shoulders.

"She's okay. There's no one else."

I take in a huge deep breath, my first one since I hit that **CALL** button. "Thank God." I sigh, which gets a soft giggle out of Gram.

"But listen," she says, her tone suddenly hushed. "I don't think we should have this conversation on the phone. Not with . . . I don't live alone, as you may recall."

I nod in understanding before it registers that Gram can't see me through the phone. "I appreciate your discretion, Gram. Are you free to meet up tomorrow to talk more?"

Her tone perks up. "I know just the place. I'll send over the address. Wanna meet there first thing in the morning, sweetie?"

We finalize our plans, and once we've said our good-byes, I end the call and am instantly hit with the world's biggest wave of relief.

Gram could have hung up on me. She could have lied and told me that they moved clear across the country. But instead, she told me what I've been desperate to hear since Claire planted the idea in my head earlier today.

Peyton isn't seeing anyone else.

And it might be a long shot, but I just might still have a chance.

After the month I've had, I think I just about forgot

what it feels like to get a good night's sleep. But this morning, when my alarm buzzed me awake, I didn't want to immediately suffocate myself with my pillow. And I have Gram to thank for that.

For the first time since Peyton and I stopped talking, I didn't have to spend the whole night fighting off nightmares about losing her. Because last night, the glimmer of hope I got from talking with Gram was enough to push my anxiety aside and let me get some rest. I should bring that woman flowers for that alone.

After a quick shower, I snag a bagel for breakfast and head for my car to meet up with Gram. Sliding into the driver's seat, I copy and paste the address she sent over last night into my GPS and hit GO, expecting a coffee shop or a diner to pop up on my screen.

Nope. Not even close.

The Painted Palette Nail Salon? That has to be a mistake. I must have only copied part of the address or something.

But after triple-checking Gram's text, calling the store to make sure the maps app is up-to-date, and clarifying with Gram that she didn't have a senior moment and sent me to the wrong spot, it's clear that I didn't make a typo. Nope. Instead, I made a date to get pampered with Peyton's grandma.

With a sigh, I buckle up, both literally and emotionally. No time to change plans now. I have a nail appointment to make and a girl to win back.

It's a quick drive to the salon, which turns out to be right down the street from Peyton and Gram's house. When I walk in, a bell on the door rings, announcing my entrance. Like I needed any more introduction as a thirty-four-year-old man walking into a nail salon. Everyone's eyes are immediately on me, so I roll back my shoulders, trying to look like this isn't my first time setting foot in one of these places.

Gram is already here, standing in front of a wall of tiny, colorful bottles of polish, running one finger along the line of different shades of purple. She's still got her walker, but I'm impressed by how little she's relying on it. No wonder Peyton is so damn unstoppable. She learned from the best.

"Oh, good, you made it!" Gram gestures for me to come hug her, so I do. She has a mischievous gleam in her eye as she nods toward the nail-polish wall. "I hope your feet are ready for a pedi. What are you thinking? Maybe pink or light blue?"

I chuckle, noting the devilish smile on her lips. Joke's on her, though. I may be a rookie in the pedicure department, but between the stress of the launch and the drama between Peyton and me, I'm due for a little R&R.

"I'm going to forgo the polish," I say. "But if pedicures are on the agenda, I'll try anything once."

At Gram's go-ahead, a pair of nail ladies from behind the counter head back to prepare what looks to be two very elaborate massage chairs with built-in tubs. Man, I must really be in for a treat.

Gram scoots her walker along the shiny white tile and toward the black leather lounge chairs in the waiting area. "Let's sit and chat. They won't be ready for us for a few more minutes."

I offer an arm to help her sit down, but she makes a point of not taking it. Like I said, the woman is unstoppable.

As I snag the seat next to her, Gram's eyes scan mine, taking in my expression of equal parts hope and anxiety.

"You miss her, don't you." A statement, not a question. She already knows the answer.

"Like crazy," I mutter under my breath. "Can

you please tell me how she's doing?"

Gram sighs, rotating her wrist back and forth in the universal sign for *so-so*. "She was bad for a while. I think she's a bit better now, but it's hard to tell with how busy she's been. I couldn't tell you the last time that girl pulled her nose out of her work since you up and left." Playfully, she elbows me in the ribs. "I guess she needs you around to balance out that work with a little play. Just like you promised me, right?"

A sad smile twitches at the corner of my mouth. I had almost forgotten about the bargain we struck back in that hotel lobby.

"I tried to keep up my end of our deal, Gram. I swear. But I guess it just complicated things. But now that I'm without her . . ." I trail off, scratching at my stubble as I try to choose my words.

Oh, to hell with it. We've made it this far. I gulp down the lump in my throat and speak my mind.

"I love your granddaughter. And I would do anything to win her back."

Gram's first response is shock, but her wide eyes and dropped jaw slowly shift into a warm smile. "Well then," she says, fisting her hands and pressing them into her hips. "I guess we have some serious planning to do, don't we?"

Just then, our nail experts return and escort us back to where the magic happens. I follow Gram's lead as she ditches her shoes before climbing into the massage chair and sinking her feet into the bubbling foot bath.

Gram and both the nail ladies laugh as I dip one toe into the tub and jerk back. Fuck, that water is hot. How the hell do women do this all the time? Better try a slower approach.

Carefully, I sink my feet one inch at a time into the churning bubbles, sucking in a breath through my teeth and slowly letting it out. Once I get a chance to adjust, it's really not so bad. And the smell of eucalyptus from whatever oils and salts are in the water is actually pretty damn soothing.

I turn and look at Gram to verify that I'm doing this right. She's relaxed in her chair, her eyes closed, a satisfied grin on her face. She must feel me looking at her, though, because the second I glance her way, she speaks up.

"So, if you're going to win back my granddaughter, you're going to have to really impress her. Show her that you're serious about her. If you can do that, I'm nearly certain she'll at least hear what you have to say." She slowly opens her eyes and gives me a skeptical look. "That is, if you can figure out how you're going to impress her. That's what we need to brainstorm on."

Before I get a chance to give it much thought, my assigned nail lady taps on my left shin, looking up at me expectantly.

"That means you're supposed to take that foot out of the tub," Gram whispers.

Who knew that nail salons came with this secret code?

I lift one foot out of the water and into the nail technician's hand. With some sort of spongy stone, she starts scrubbing at my heel, causing me to squirm in my seat, holding back a laugh.

"I'm ticklish," I say apologetically.

"You really are a pedicure rookie." Gram giggles so hard that she snorts. It takes her a second to collect herself, but when she does, her giggles are long gone, replaced with a completely serious expression.

"Now you have to be honest with me, dear," she says, her voice low and stern. "Are you in this for the long haul? Things always find a way to get tough sometimes. I can't have you running out on my girl when times are too hard. She deserves better than that."

I nod soberly in agreement. "If she'll have me, I won't be going anywhere. She's all I want in this world right now."

Gram raises a brow in my direction. "Just right now?"

"No, not just right now," I say, correcting myself. "Forever."

CHAPTER TWENTY-SIX

Peyton

When I walk into the kitchen, I can hardly see Gram through the enormous cloud of lemon-scented cleaning spray in the air. She's been on a cleaning spree since the second she finished her coffee this morning.

"Hey there, Mr. Clean. Everything okay?"

"Fine, fine," she mutters, giving the counter another wipe down, despite the fact that it's already glistening. "Just getting things ready for when Duncan arrives."

Since the doctors cleared Gram to only use her walker as needed, she's spent nearly every waking moment on her feet.

"Let me get that." I reach out to stop Gram from trying to lift a mop bucket full of soapy water.

"No, no, don't worry about it. You go get ready."

I scrunch my nose. Get ready? For what? I was kind of planning on rocking this yoga pants and oversized sweatshirt look for most of the day. I'll just be catching up on emails and watching TV all day.

Before I can ask her to clarify, Gram has already moved on to deep cleaning the outside of the dishwasher with quick, aggressive scrubs. She's a woman on a mission.

The dishwasher doesn't keep her attention for long, though. As I head for the fridge to size up my snack options, I can feel Gram's stare on my back, giving me a thorough once-over.

"What's wrong?" I call over my shoulder. "Is there a stain on my sweatshirt or something?"

"I just think you should put on something a little nicer," she says. "You know, maybe throw on some makeup, do your hair."

I close the fridge and turn to face Gram, folding my arms over my chest. "What's the deal? You're acting weird."

"No, I'm not," she says, her tone suddenly defensive. "We're just having company, that's all."

"Duncan hardly counts as company at this point, Gram," I say with an eye roll. "And I doubt that he would care if I'm in yoga pants or not."

Gram sticks out her bottom lip and gives me her best puppy-dog eyes. "It would mean a lot to me if, just this once, you looked a little nicer, okay? It's important to me."

Ugh. I don't know what she has up her sleeve today, but I can't say no to my own grandmother pouting at me.

"Fine." I sigh. "I'll change if it makes you happy." The old lady is clearly going senile.

Gram's face brightens with an enthusiastic smile, and without another word, she shoos me out of the kitchen and back up the stairs.

Jeez. Whatever date she has planned with Duncan must be good if she's being this crazy about making a good impression. He's seen me after a full night of sobbing over Josh. Compared to that morning, I look photo-shoot ready right now. But if it's that important to her, I'll swap out the yoga pants for a proper pair of jeans. At least until Duncan leaves. Then I'm going right back to yoga pants.

Normally my getting-ready routine takes thirty minutes, forty-five if I'm going to wash and blow-dry my hair, which today, I am. Gram has unleashed enough aerosol on this house today. I don't need to contribute my dry shampoo to that health hazard.

Once I'm all toweled off and blow-dried, I pick out a ruby-red sweater that Gram bought for me last Christmas and shimmy on a pair of jeans. Nice jeans, not my favorite comfy ones that have well-placed holes in the knees. Just as I'm swiping on my favorite peachy lip gloss, the doorbell rings. Perfect timing.

"Can you get that?" Gram yells from somewhere downstairs. "I'm in the middle of something."

First she makes me change, now I'm playing doorman? Duncan better be at the door with the Queen of England at this rate. I giggle to myself as I imagine myself trying to figure out how to curtsy.

"Coming!" I call out as I head down the stairs two at a time. Fall is coming to a close, and I don't want to leave Duncan out in the cold.

"Hey, Dunc—"

I've got half a sentence out by the time I've swung the door all the way open, welcoming today's surprise visitor. No, not the Queen of England. This guest is far more nerve-racking.

Josh Hanson is standing on my front porch, two bouquets of flowers in his arms.

Am I hallucinating from all the cleaning products I've been breathing in?

What the hell is he doing here? I've just barely started considering the idea of getting over him. And that's already been hard enough.

I find myself sputtering like a car that won't start, unable to form a sentence, not even a word. I must look ridiculous, standing here with my eyes wide as the color drains from my cheeks. Ninety percent of me wants to slam the door and sprint back upstairs to the safety of my bedroom.

But I don't slam the door. Because there's still ten percent of me that, for some twisted reason, is fucking rejoicing that he's here.

We stand there for a moment, staring at each other until he finally breaks the silence.

"These are for you." He nods toward one of the

bouquets—half red roses, half sunflowers. They're absolutely gorgeous.

"Is the other one for some other girl?" I snap, my throat closing up a little more with each syllable.

Josh snickers. "They're for Gram. I don't think she counts as some other girl."

Damn it. Duh, Peyton. Get it together.

Right on cue, Gram walks up behind me and lays a reassuring hand on my shoulder. Spotting the flowers, she coos in delight. "So sweet of you, Josh. But you didn't have to get me anything."

"Of course I did. You helped me coordinate this, after all."

I plant my hands firmly on my hips. So *that* is what's happening here. Gram got sick of my moping and took the situation into her own hands.

"So Gram got to you, huh?" There's venom in my voice, and I don't even bother trying to sweeten it up.

He shakes his head. "No, I reached out to her. I wanted to check on you. Do you mind if I come in?"

The question is directed entirely at me, but I don't have a clue how to answer it.

Do I mind? Did I mind when he disappeared from my life for two weeks? Did I mind when he randomly showed up at my favorite bar and ruined my celebration with my friends? Of course I mind. A bouquet of flowers isn't going to make all of that disappear.

But the man I had all but given my whole heart to is standing here, on my front porch, clearly after talking to Gram about it. And that ten percent within me that doesn't hate him, the part that wants to absolutely leap into his arms and kiss him again and again, takes control.

"Come on in."

"No, no," Gram says, reaching out to take the flowers from Josh's arms. "I'll get these in water. You two go have fun."

I swivel my head around, squinting at Gram. Go have fun? What are we, first graders on a play-date?

"I did have somewhere in mind, if you're up to it," Josh says. "Scoops? On me?"

I look back at Gram, who's smiling, her eyes

urging me forward. Clearly, she knows something I don't. And whatever it is, I want to find out. Which is going to mean taking a leap of faith and listening what Josh has to say.

Sucking in a deep breath, I hold it, weighing my options carefully, and then sigh my response. "Let me get my coat."

The drive to Scoops is silent and short, and it's not until we arrive that it clicks that it's a bit cold for ice cream. The totally empty tables are evidence of that. It's also only eleven in the morning, but stepping into the location of one of our first dates / business meetings unleashes the butterflies in my stomach all over again.

As I snag the same table we had last time, Josh walks straight to the counter, where I expect him to place an order for two chocolate-dipped cones. To my surprise, he asks if it's possible to make chocolate-dipped ice cream in a dish. The woman behind the counter laughs, but agrees that for a regular like Josh, anything is possible.

When he takes his seat, pushing one dish of ice cream across the table to me, I finally get the opportunity to take him in. Underneath his black jacket, the blue Henley stretched tight across his chest makes his eyes absolutely sparkle. He's as handsome as ever, although maybe a bit more tired than usual. Maybe he hasn't been sleeping well either since we split.

"So, why the dish and not the cone?" I ask, suspiciously taking my first bite.

"I don't want you to get your hands all covered in ice cream, because I have something to give you."

"A written apology?" I tease.

"Not quite."

Slipping a hand into his coat pocket, he pulls out a gold envelope with my name neatly printed on the front. He places it on the table between us, but as I lean forward to grab it, he reaches out a hand and lays it gently on top of mine, sending sparks dancing through me. I can't believe one little touch can still affect me like that.

"Before you open it, though," Josh says in a low voice. "I have something I need to say."

"I'm listening." I lift my chin, waiting.

"First, I want to apologize. There's been a lot of miscommunication between us, and it's been really unfair to you." He has a tremor in his voice, a vulnerability that shakes me to my core. He really is sorry.

"Well, I want an explanation, that much is for sure." I fiddle nervously with my ice cream spoon, dodging his eye contact.

"And I'll give you one," he says. "But first, open the envelope. Please."

After taking a deep breath, I slide my thumb underneath the seal and pull two sets of airplane tickets from the envelope. New York to Buffalo. First class. They're for this June.

"What? I . . ." I run my fingers over the glossy finish of the tickets, trying to make sense of them. "Is this a work trip or something?"

"No, Peyton." Josh laughs. "We're not going for business this time. I don't want this to be a professional relationship anymore. I want to take you upstate the right way. Not as my business partner. As my girlfriend."

My heart jolts in my chest. His *girlfriend*. I've wanted to hear him call me that since the day I first laid eyes on him.

"And these other two?" I ask, counting the tickets again. There are four.

"For Gram and Duncan. They already have it

marked on their calendars. Gram seems to be healing well, but the flights are accessible in case she's having any walking issues come June. We can take Gram and Duncan to all the wineries. And we can swing by Claire's and see the kids." He grabs my hand again, giving it a gentle squeeze. "Our families can meet. If you want, that is."

The thought of Gram sitting on a swing, snapping pictures of Claire's kids while Duncan chases them around the yard, brings a smile to my face. It's a picture-perfect moment. One that almost seems too good to be true.

I look at the tickets again, splaying them out in front of me for closer examination.

"But these flights aren't until June," I say, suddenly skeptical. "Summer is so far away, and you don't know—"

"That's where you're wrong. I do know. I know that I want to be with you this summer and next summer and for as many summers as you'll have me." A gentle smile creeps across his lips.

I want to kiss that smile more than anything. But there's still one more thing to clarify first.

"But what about these past few weeks? What was that? What happened?"

Josh's shoulders sag. "These past few weeks without you have been hell on fuckin' earth, Peyton. But it was all a misunderstanding. When I was taken off as the point of contact for the project, it's because Brody thought that I was biased about your business, that I only thought it would succeed because I was so into you. So I backed off the project to prove to him that my feelings for you and work were separate. But then Brody didn't give you the details of that, and . . ."

He sighs again, shaking his head as he worries his fingers through his messy dark hair. "God, Peyton, I was such a jackass. I'm so sorry. I thought you knew. And then I showed up at Speakeasy, thinking you'd be excited to see me. I'm sorry about that."

His defeat hangs in the air between us for a moment as I let his words soak in.

"That sounds so complicated," I say finally. "So Brody didn't tell me because . . ."

Josh scoffs, shaking his head. "Because he's a man, I suppose. We can tend to get a little stupid on details and emotions sometimes. Especially when a beautiful woman is involved."

A smile twitches the corner of my mouth. I grab his hand again, giving it an extra-tight squeeze.

"You were smart enough to know you screwed up. And you were smart enough to book this trip. Which is just about the sweetest thing anyone has ever done for me."

Josh perks up, the weight disappearing from his shoulders. "So you'll go?"

Leaning across the table, I press a light, delicate kiss against his lips. "With you? I'd go just about anywhere." I pause, still leaning halfway across the table. "Well, on one condition."

Josh raises a brow at me.

"As long as we don't have to keep it professional," I say, grinning.

He laughs, taking my cheek in his hand and bringing his lips to mine again. "Peyton, falling in love with you is the least professional thing I've ever done. And I want to keep doing it over and over again."

EPILOGUE

Peyton

It's been a year, almost to the day, since I rushed out of the Wine O'Clock office after my very first meeting with Josh. Three hundred sixty-five days, give or take, since the moment that redefined what it meant to be nervous. My business was on the brink of something incredible, something possibly life changing, and life decided to throw a monkey wrench in the situation in the form of a misdirected text message and a business partner almost too swoon worthy for me to keep my eyes on my goals.

And now, with a whole year of ups and downs behind us, I can say without the slightest doubt that Josh still gives me the same fluttery feeling in my stomach that he did the first day I met him. Only now, I know better than to think it's nerves. It's excitement. Because I've found the man I'll spend the rest of my life with.

Today, after years of dating my way through douchebags and noncommittal jerks, it's finally my day to wear white.

Well, to be clear, it's not *only* my day. Josh and I aren't the only couple sharing our first dance underneath the twinkling winery lights tonight. We're toasting to true love with the other cutest couple the state of New York has to offer—Gram and Duncan.

To this day, both Josh and Duncan swear that they never discussed their individual plans to propose this summer. On our trip upstate, when Josh got down on one knee in the middle of the most gorgeous winery in town, Duncan laughed, pulled a ring from his pocket, and did the same.

It was the kind of moment I always thought was reserved only for fairy tales, and yet there we were, Gram and me, saying yes to our forevers. Now, four months later, we're back at the same winery, surrounded by family and friends as we wind down an evening of dancing and wine drinking in celebration of saying *I do*.

"Hey, lovebirds!" Sabrina's lavender bridesmaid dress is bunched up in one hand to keep her from tripping as she shimmies toward the dance floor. Libby is only a few paces behind her.

For a few moments, I gaze out at our friends and family on the dance floor. Claire is dancing with her husband, and Brody has one of Josh's nieces in his arms. Warm satisfaction pulses through me as I watch them.

I turn toward Josh, half to gauge his reaction and half as an excuse to take in how freaking handsome my husband looks in his tux. Because *damn*. The man is fine. And he's all mine.

He hasn't been this dressed up since the infamous night at the hotel event last year. The night that started it all between us. Unless, well, you count the night I opened my texts to find the world's most unexpected surprise.

"What do you think, babe?" I ask my brand-new hubby, gesturing toward the dance floor. "Should we join them?"

Josh shrugs and gives me a sweet kiss on the cheek. "Whatever you want, Mrs. Hanson."

A proud blush blooms on my cheeks. I'm so happy to finally be officially his. After sneaking one last sidelong glance at my gorgeous husband, I lift my glass of wine from the table, and settle in at his side. "I think I'm all danced out."

The song changes, and a familiar jazzy intro floats through the air. It only takes three or four notes for Gram to recognize the song and jump to her feet, clapping her hands in excitement.

"Our song!" she squeals, snagging Duncan's hand. "Come on, guys. We gotta get down to this one."

Gram and Duncan head out to the dance floor, leaving Josh and me hanging back at the table to watch them get their groove on.

Under the white linen tablecloth, I feel Josh's hand shift and find its grip on my thigh, giving me a quick squeeze through the tulle of my wedding dress. A tingle of heat creeps along my spine. We've been public about our relationship for a long time now, but there's still something incredibly sexy about stealing a secret kiss or a hidden touch here and there.

"Do you think anyone would notice if we slipped out of here and headed to our room a little early?" Josh whispers near my ear, his hushed tone barely loud enough for me to hear over the music.

I hide my smile as I think over his offer. We rented out the winery's whole bed and breakfast for our guests, and it's only a short walk away. We could be under the covers and tangled up in each other by the end of this song, if we're fast.

"I think we might be able to make a clean exit. Why? Got something on your mind?"

Josh shakes his head and chuckles. "Oh, Mrs. Hanson. I've had a few things on my mind since the moment I laid eyes on you today."

"Oh yeah?" I challenge him, playfully teasing my lower lip with the tip of my tongue. "And what might those be?"

"Well, number one, I haven't been able to stop thinking about how I'm the single luckiest man on the planet," he says. "And, number two, although that dress is absolutely stunning on you, I haven't for half a second stopped thinking about taking it off of you."

A quiver dances between my thighs. I guess that's all the convincing I need.

As the music crescendos and the guests on the dance floor get even rowdier, I lay my hand in Josh's, taking a second to admire the gorgeous sparkly rock on my finger before letting him tug me to my feet. In one swift movement, he pulls me into a sweet, tender kiss that leaves me as breathless as ever.

I will never get tired of kissing this man. Thank God I have the rest of my life to do it.

"C'mon, baby," he says coyly, lacing his fingers through mine. "Now's our chance. Let's get out of here."

Our stealthy exit consists mostly of ducking behind caterers and drunk relatives, but it's hard not to be noticed at your own wedding. Gram spots me from the dance floor and gives me an encouraging wink and a wave good-bye as we make our final escape. By the time we stumble into our room at the B&B, we're both a mess of giggles and stolen kisses.

"God, I love you, Josh Hanson." I sigh into the crook of his neck as his fingers work to unbutton my dress.

"I love you too, Peyton."

As we fall into bed, Josh still in his tux and me in nothing but my lacy white panties and bra, I pull back momentarily from his kiss to pose the question that's been on my mind for some time now.

"Babe? When we have kids, how are we going to tell them we met?"

Josh snickers, then pauses to give it some serious thought. "I guess we should probably leave out the part where I accidentally sent you a picture of my dick, right?"

"No shit." I laugh, pressing a kiss against the line of his jaw. "I suppose we could just say we met at work, right?"

"Well, I'm not sure that would make us sound very *professional*, now would it?"

Josh squeezes my side and we both erupt into laughter again. We spend the next ten minutes offering up different phallic excuses, saying we bumped into each other buying bananas at the grocery store or at a Mets game waiting in line for hot dogs.

After plenty of giggles, Josh finally snaps his fingers, a devilish look in his eyes.

"I've got it," he says with a wicked smile. "We'll just tell them a message from me popped up in your junk mail."

I hoped you enjoyed Josh & Peyton's story!
Up next is a decidedly *steamy* book called
THE TWO-WEEK ARRANGEMENT with

some majorly angsty vibes. Dominic Aspen is a grumpy-pants CEO single dad to twin little girls, who has zero time or inclination for a flirtation with his girl-next-door-type intern, Presley. But she's never been very good at following instructions. Read an exclusive sneak preview on the next page.

THE
TWO WEEK
Arrangement

Exclusive Preview

"You don't have to be uncomfortable."

She nearly jumps at the sound of my voice.

Nice work, Dom.

"Don't I?" Presley asks, laughing softly.

"I understand if you are."

"No, I . . . I'm uncomfortable with how easy it was."

"How do you mean?"

"Sitting there, talking business. Flattering the client. Being your date."

There's that word again. Why don't I want to correct her when she uses it?

"You were good at it," I say in a low voice. Arousal stirs in my veins, and I take a breath to remind myself why this is a terrible idea.

"Thank you," she says with a soft smile. Even in the dark of the limo, I can see her eyes sparkle. "It was my first time. Doing something like this, I mean."

She's a good girl, just as I suspected. She's probably never broken one rule, done anything outside of her straight-A, Miss Responsible routine in her entire life. So, why does that thought make me want to bend her over my desk and spank her ass?

"Really? I couldn't tell," I say, trying to keep my tone cool.

"No, I just wasn't sure how it would go. Pretending with you, I mean," she says, wringing her hands. "I'm sorry, I shouldn't be so chatty about this with you. Duh."

She's so fucking cute.

"It's no trouble. I'm interested."

"Well, thanks. I'm glad you were my first." She blushes immediately. "Can you pretend I didn't just say that?"

"Sure."

I say one thing, but as usual, my body does another. My cock sure can't forget that little piece of treasured knowledge.

This dinner was incredibly successful on the business front. Not exactly a personal victory for the front of my pants, however. I'm still as horny as fuck, if not more than before. *Goddammit.*

We pull up to her apartment complex. I climb out of the car, walk around, and open her door. She quietly steps out. The distance between us is maddening, but I maintain it all the same.

"Have a good night," she says softly, almost breathless.

Am I making you nervous, Presley?

"You're not done with me yet." I offer her my arm.

"Oh, I'm not—"

"Don't worry. I just want to walk you to your door."

"Oh. All right." She bites her lip, stifling a soft laugh, as she loops her arm through mine.

I can't remember the last time I walked a woman to her door. It should bother me that this feels much more like a date than It should. Presley's my employee for Christ's sake. But I guess I'm still riding a high of how well she did winning over Roger.

We walk in silence up to her apartment door. It reminds me of where I lived in college, an old brick and mortar with a buzzer next to the door. Nostalgia fills me with a thousand memories of the younger me. Bold. Reckless. Carefree.

It seems like a lifetime ago.

I hold her hand up the steps until we reach the top, enjoying how soft her skin is as it rests lightly against my palm. At the door, she turns back to me. I'm on the stair below, our eyes at the same level. For a moment, we just take in the sight of each other. She really is beautiful with her high cheekbones, wide eyes, and full mouth.

"Thank you, Dominic. I had a nice time." It's almost a whisper. She isn't quite looking in my eyes anymore, but rather her gaze rests on my lips.

Interesting.

"No. Thank you," I say softly.

Her hand is still in mine, and I lift it to the lips she's been staring at to press a chaste kiss to the back of her hand. I swear I can feel her take in a breath. With my lips still touching her, I meet her eyes.

A blush spreads across her cheeks. "See you at work," I murmur.

Moments later, I climb into the limo. I settle into my seat, watching as Presley unlocks her apartment door and steps inside.

"Home, sir?" my driver asks.

"Yes, home."

Acknowledgements

I would like to thank you, dear sweet reader, for picking up a copy of this book. I hope you enjoyed it! I feel so blessed to dream up love stories for you to enjoy.

An immense thank you to my editing team of Elaine York and Pam Berehulke who were so instrumental in helping shape this story. I would like to thank the fabulous Lauren Blakely with a special wink for your thoughts and enthusiasm on the early versions of this story. I'm so lucky to know you!

Thank you to my incredible assistant and right hand in all the things, Alyssa Garcia from Uplifting Designs and Marketing for your support and constant cheerfulness as we tackle well, *everything* that this industry throws our way. You are one of the hardest working women I know, and I'm proud to be on this journey with you.

To my sweet husband John for all the back rubs, the laughs and the sushi rolls over which we dream together. And thank you for never once rolling your eyes, no matter how cuckoo-bananas my ideas are. You're the reason I can do what I do. If behind every strong man is a stronger woman, then the reverse is true too.

Last but not least, thank you Jesus for blessing me so immensely!

Get Two Free Books

Sign up for my newsletter and I'll automatically send you two free books.

www.kendallryanbooks.com/newsletter

Follow Kendall

BookBub has a feature where you can follow me and get an alert when I release a book or put a title on sale. Sign up here to stay in the loop:

www.bookbub.com/authors/kendall-ryan

Website

www.kendallryanbooks.com

Facebook

www.facebook.com/kendallryanbooks

Twitter

www.twitter.com/kendallryan1

Instagram

www.instagram.com/kendallryan1

Newsletter

www.kendallryanbooks.com/newsletter

About the Author

A *New York Times*, *Wall Street Journal*, and *USA TODAY* bestselling author of more than two dozen titles, Kendall Ryan has sold over two million books, and her books have been translated into several languages in countries around the world. Her books have also appeared on the *New York Times* and *USA TODAY* bestseller list more than three dozen times. Kendall has been featured in publications such as *USA TODAY*, *Newsweek*, and *In Touch Magazine*. She lives in Texas with her husband and two sons.

To be notified of new releases or sales, join Kendall's private Mailing List.

www.kendallryanbooks.com/newsletter

Get even more of the inside scoop when you join Kendall's private Facebook group, Kendall's Kinky Cuties:

www.facebook.com/groups/kendallskinkycuties

Other Books by Kendall Ryan

Unravel Me

Filthy Beautiful Lies Series

The Room Mate

The Play Mate

The House Mate

The Impact of You

Screwed

The Fix Up

Dirty Little Secret

xo, Zach

Baby Daddy

Tempting Little Tease

Bro Code

Love Machine

Flirting with Forever

Dear Jane

Finding Alexei

Boyfriend for Hire

The Two Week Arrangement

For a complete list of Kendall's books, visit:

www.kendallryanbooks.com/all-books/

CPSIA information can be obtained
at www.ICGtesting.com
Printed in the USA
LVHW050333020519
616374LV00003B/90/P